This man ha~~~~~~
grievously.

She *knew* she was e~~~~~~ ~~~~ a place in medical school. Neil had rejected her without good cause. Now she found herself working with him, even going to dinner with him. She was discovering that under that spiky exterior there was a man who could be witty, charming, thoughtful. She really liked him, even. . .

Her life had been easier when he'd been just an object of her hate.

Gill Sanderson is a psychologist who finds time to write only by staying up late at night. Weekends are filled by her hobbies of gardening, running and mountain walking. Her ideas come from her work, from one son who is an oncologist, one son who is a nurse and her daughter, who is a trainee midwife. She first wrote articles for learned journals and chapters for a textbook. Then she was encouraged to change to fiction by her husband, who is an established writer of war stories.

Recent titles by the same author:

DR RYDER AND SON
COUNTRY DOCTORS

LAKELAND
NURSE

BY
GILL SANDERSON

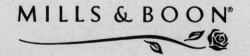

MILLS & BOON®

To Liz, Celia, John and all in Room 115.

*First published in Great Britain 1997
Harlequin Mills & Boon Limited,
Eton House, 18-24 Paradise Road, Richmond, Surrey TW9 1SR*

© Gill Sanderson 1997

ISBN 0 263 80053 9

*Set in Times 10 on 12 pt. by
Rowland Phototypesetting Limited
Bury St Edmunds, Suffolk*

03-9703-45819-D

*Printed and bound in Great Britain
by Mackays of Chatham PLC, Chatham*

CHAPTER ONE

FOR Zanne the day had started with a shock.

When she'd come down that morning her mother had, as usual, made breakfast for her. Zanne had long ago given up arguing; her mother said that she was perfectly able to cook in her own kitchen now that it had been specially adapted for wheelchair use. Besides, it kept her active and Elizabeth Ripley hated not to be busy.

But that wasn't the shock.

'You're doing what?' Zanne asked incredulously.

Elizabeth smiled. 'I'm going to Canada for six months. Joe's brother's family have invited him over to stay, and he's said he'll go if he can bring me.'

'But how will you. . .? Just the two of you. . . I mean you're not. . .'

Elizabeth's bright blue eyes sparkled. 'It's mothers who are supposed to say that to daughters, not the other way round,' she said mischievously. 'It'll all be perfectly proper; we're going to get married. How d'you fancy being a bridesmaid?'

'Oh, Mum!' With tears in her eyes, Zanne leaned over the steel arm of the wheelchair and hugged her mother's erect figure. 'I think it's wonderful!'

Her mother had met Joe Oldham two years ago when he'd come to the wheelchair dancing club that she had set up. Like Elizabeth, Joe had found himself confined to a wheelchair after a fall. Again like her, he had determined not to let it ruin his life. He'd kept his garage business going and had a car specially adapted so that he could still drive.

Zanne had noticed that the two had been seeing quite a lot of each other, visiting theatres, concerts and restaurants, but she hadn't realised that things had gone this far. 'I think Joe's a marvellous man.'

Elizabeth nodded. 'Some day I hope you do as well, my dear. When your father died, and you were so small, I doubted that I'd ever look at another man. But I have and I'm happy. Now—' Elizabeth pointed at the plate '—eat your breakfast or you'll be late for work!'

'I hope Joe knows what a slave-driver he's marrying!' Zanne grinned and picked up her knife and fork.

An hour later her delight was still with her, but tucked away in the back of her mind. Time to start work on Ward 17—Male Orthopaedics. As ever, there was that feeling of exhilaration and anticipation. What would the day bring?

The first thing she saw as she hurried down the corridor was Mickey Dent, a seventeen-year-old clad in jeans and a lurid T-shirt. Mickey was making slow but definite progress on his crutches.

'How about this, Zanne?' he shouted as she drew near. 'Another twenty feet travelled today.'

'You're doing well, Mickey,' she replied, 'but don't push too hard. Stick to what the doctor says you are to do and you'll be out quicker.'

'That's me. I'm bored stiff here; I want to get back to work. Don't forget, you promised to come out with me on my bike when I can walk.'

'I did no such thing!' she protested, smiling.

Mickey and his motorbike had hit a kerb at seventy miles an hour. The bike was, unfortunately, undamaged. Mickey had been knocked unconscious, had suffered abrasions to his upper torso and had sustained comminuted fractures to both tibia and fibula. It had taken a long, patient session in Theatre before Mickey's bones had been put together adequately.

'I'll come for a ride with you if you buy a car,' she offered.

'Ah, Zanne, you sound just like my ma.'

Zanne grinned. One of the good things about working on an orthopaedic ward was that she often saw impressive results. She remembered seeing the X-ray of Mickey's leg and thinking that no surgeon could ever put it together. But one had.

Mickey, surprisingly, had been a model patient, suffering obvious pain with fortitude and never trying to take his misery out on the staff. She wished that all patients could be like him. She also wished that he would sell his bike.

'Morning, Zanne,' her friend, Sister Mary Kelly, said. 'We're one short again. Student nurse off with flu.'

Zanne grimaced. There was never enough cover. If a nurse was off then the rest of the staff would have to work harder. 'We'll cope,' she said. 'I'll—' She broke off as the buzzer sounded. They both looked at the board.

Beside every bed there was an emergency buzzer, which signalled in the sister's office. Most patients used it with consideration, knowing that the staff was hard pressed. Some did not.

'Edgar Grant,' Mary said. 'We both know there's nothing wrong with him.'

'I'll go,' said Zanne. 'Let's see what Edgar is bored with now.'

Edgar Grant had tripped, coming out of a pub, late one night. He was half-drunk. He had fallen, stiff-armed, and had suffered a fracture of the left humerus. After reduction, the surgeon had put the arm in traction. Edgar wasn't in any pain but the traction was inconvenient and Edgar didn't like being inconvenienced.

'Nurse, this sling is causing me no end of pain. Can't you do anything with it?'

In fact, there was nothing that Zanne could do because she knew that he had no pain. However, she rearranged her patient so that he would suffer minimum irritation, tidied his bed and smoothed his pillow.

'If you can just lie like this, Mr Grant, you should find things get easier.'

'I hope so. My solicitor's coming to see me this afternoon, Nurse. We're going to sue, you know.' Mr Grant smiled self-importantly. 'People don't fool with me.'

'I'm sure they don't, Mr Grant.' Zanne fled.

'Sometimes I think I'd like to transfer to Gynae,' Zanne grumbled to Mary as they reviewed the day's work. 'The mums have something to occupy their minds—new babies. The trouble with this ward is that everyone gets bored.'

'That's Orthopaedics,' Mary agreed philosophically. 'What we need is more ill people.'

It was a problem on their ward. Many of their patients weren't actually ill—they'd just broken bones and so had to lie still. And some, especially the younger ones, didn't have the inner resources to cope, so they took it out on the staff. Zanne and Mary had learned to deal with this. Their little grumble wasn't serious—it was just a way of dealing with the pressure.

After breakfast there was the drug round. Mostly the patients needed painkillers—though some needed treatment for conditions other than broken bones. This was a good chance for Zanne to have a friendly word with everybody. She noticed as she passed Mr Grant that he was no longer lying in the position she had suggested.

Then there were dressings and inspection for bed-sores. Because patients had to lie still so long bedsores were a particular danger in this ward. Zanne rubbed a couple of suspect areas with lanolin cream, ordered pads for a pensioner's spine and elbow and put a granu-flex patch on a sore coccyx. They had just one patient on an airflow bed and she gently checked his condition. He was comfortable.

'Staff, could you help me with Mr Aston, please?' An occupational therapist appeared behind Zanne. 'He seems a bit reluctant.'

Mr Aston was another pensioner who had just had a hip replacement. This was to be his first attempt at putting weight on his new joint. Zanne appreciated his concern—it didn't seem long since he had been in Theatre.

Carefully the two manoeuvred him so that he was sitting on the edge of the bed. Then they eased him upright. He was obviously nervous, but Zanne encouraged him. 'We don't want you going for a run, Mr Aston—at least not yet. Now, we're just going to let go of you—don't worry, we're right here. OK? How does that feel?'

A great smile spread over the old man's face. 'It doesn't feel too bad, Nurse—not too bad at all.'

'We'll have you in a marathon yet. But, now, just a couple of steps and then back into bed.'

Occasions like seeing Mr Aston smile made Zanne's job worthwhile.

In the middle of the morning there was a new admission, one that Zanne had been dreading. Jimmy Prenton, aged sixteen, came in with his mother. He had osteosarcoma of the lower end of the femur. Bone cancer. Zanne knew that the limb would have to be amputated and then there would be a programme of cytotoxic drugs to inhibit any possible spreading of the cancer. Even so, the prognosis wasn't good.

She completed the necessary admissions procedure, noting Jimmy's valiant attempt to keep cheerful. Then she took his mother to the sister's office for a talk. They would be seeing a lot of each other.

It had been a hard morning but satisfying—typical, in fact. At lunchtime she decided not to go to the canteen. She would have a coffee and a biscuit in the sister's office. She slipped off her shoes and rested her feet on Mary's chair.

There was a knock on the door; her heart sank. If you were in the office you were on duty. It was her own fault; she should have gone to the canteen. Then the door opened and a blond head and handsome face appeared. Zanne's heart lurched a little. It was Charles—never Charlie—Hurst. He was, she supposed, her boyfriend. Charles was a stickler for proprieties on the ward and right now his unsmiling face indicated that he was being a doctor, not a lover.

'Ah, Staff. Having a coffee, I see.' It was curt and unnecessary; he knew that this was her lunch-break. But she'd learned to live with his little ways.

However, she was careful not to rise or put her feet down. 'Can I help you, Dr Hurst?'

'We've come to see Lewis Ellis. Could you get his case notes?'

Just for a moment she was tempted to say, when I've finished my coffee, but she didn't. She found the notes and stepped into the corridor.

Lewis Ellis was a young man of eighteen, a fanatical keep-fit enthusiast. He was a runner and a weight-trainer. He'd been running when a car, driven by two joy-riders, had smashed into him. His leg had been broken and was now in traction.

There was another man in the corridor, also in a white coat. Zanne looked at him and then turned and looked at Charles until he was forced to mutter, 'This is Dr Calder, Staff. He's interested in Ellis's case.'

Since this appeared to be the only introduction that Zanne was likely to get she extended her hand and said, 'Staff Nurse Ripley. Pleased to meet you, Dr Calder.'

He had a firm, but not brutal, grip. A tiny quirk at the side of his mouth indicated that he had noted the byplay between her and Charles.

For a moment Zanne stood and looked at the two men in front of her. Charles was fairly tall; Calder was taller. Charles's hair was burnished and carefully cut blond; Calder had short, dark hair and a widow's peak. Charles was fantastically good-looking—had he been a woman he would have been called beautiful. Calder's face was striking, rather than handsome. He had high cheek-bones, heavy brows and a muscular jaw. His lips were tight, and only his grey eyes hinted at humour or softness.

Perhaps it was the set of his shoulders or the directness of his unsmiling gaze, but there was an aura of hardness about him. This man would get what he wanted. Certainly he appeared to dominate Charles.

With a jerk she realised that he'd just spoken to her. His voice was what she might have guessed—deep and controlled. And musical.

'I'm sorry to interrupt your lunch-break, Staff, and I know you're busy. But if it would be possible to look through the notes and then have a word with this young man, I'd be very grateful.'

'There's no need for you to come down, Staff,' Charles put in.

That's me put in my place, she thought.

But Dr Calder said, 'I have a couple of questions which a nurse can answer best, if you don't mind. How is this young man coping with missing his exercises?'

'With great difficulty. He hates to be still. He worked out some arm and chest exercises, but we had to stop him doing them as we thought he was shaking his leg. When we told him he was slowing his rate of recovery he stopped at once. Now he spends all his time thinking about what he's going to do to the two joy-riders who knocked him down. I hope it's all fantasy.'

Dr Calder smiled and it altered his face completely. The forbidding look disappeared and there was someone who was—well, very attractive. Zanne hoped that he might be coming to work on her ward.

'Would you say his rate of recovery is faster than, say, a non-exercising youth?'

'Definitely. Not only has he a very positive attitude but his body seems to heal more quickly.'

'That's very interesting. Thank you, Staff.'

This time she was dismissed. She wondered who he was. He didn't seem like a doctor, which she knew was silly. It was something to do with the way he walked. She watched the two talking to Lewis Ellis and wondered what they wanted. She thought that Charles might have managed to have a quick private word with her, but he didn't.

When the two had gone she walked over to talk to Lewis.

'Nice chap, that Dr Calder,' Lewis said. 'Knows an awful lot about exercise. Said he'd look up some breathing exercises I could do, and suggest them to the consultant.'

'Nice of him,' Zanne said, 'Did you. . .'

'Staff, Mr Grant wants you—urgently.' It was the student nurse.

'I'll bet he does,' groaned Zanne, and strode away.

At half past two that afternoon Mary poked her head round the curtains of a bed and had to order Zanne to leave. 'You'll barely have time to change, as it is. And, Zanne—' Mary winked merrily '—you can do it. I know you've got it in you.'

'I don't know, Mary, I really don't. But I'm going to try.' Zanne swept her long-legged way down the ward, forcing herself to ignore the controlled urgency around her. Just for once she had to think solely of herself.

In the little cloakroom she unpinned her cap, wriggled out of the blue uniform and kicked off the sensible pumps. She only had time for the shortest of showers, and then from her locker she took a crisp white blouse and a light grey suit—the product of four hours' agonising in the High Street stores last week.

Her long black hair was tied back in its usual tight plait; she'd decided to leave it that way. A quick dab of lipstick and she was ready. First, however, she stood in front of the long mirror and deliberately checked her appearance. She remembered a tutor saying in her first year that the more urgent a job was the more important it was that you did it methodically, and checked your work afterwards.

Zanne stared critically at her reflection and then allowed herself a small smile. The suit was well cut and only hinted at her generous breasts. She looked calm, efficient, professional. If this dress didn't do the trick—well, she'd have to try appearing in a bikini and a sombrero. The passing lunatic thought made her grin broadly. Successfully repressing the butterflies in her stomach, she walked out of the door.

Belham Hospital was a large modern block, financed by the NHS. To one side of it was a graceful Georgian building—the original Belham Hall—which now held the medical teaching section of the University of the North. Feeling that her journey was somehow symbolic, Zanne walked along the glassed-in corridor that linked the two buildings. Outside, the March sunlight sparkled hopefully.

There was a different atmosphere in the entrance hall of the old house. Instead of light pastel walls there was dark wooden panelling, and a deep red carpet instead

of the hygienic vinyl found in the hospital corridors.
And something else—compared with the busy muted
hum in the hospital, this place was silent.

'May I help you?' A middle-aged secretary, cool
and efficient in heavy horn-rimmed glasses, suddenly
appeared from behind a half-open door.

Zanne stammered, 'M-my name is Suzanne Ripley;
I'm here to be interviewed—for medical training.'

'Of course, Miss Ripley.' From somewhere a tiny
notebook was produced, and Zanne's name duly noted.
'I am Miss Hope, the admission tutor's private secretary. I'm afraid Dr Dawkins has been called away.
He leaves his apologies and will be with you as soon
as he possibly can. Now I know you must be nervous
so, if you'd like to wait in here, I'll fetch you some
coffee.'

It was good coffee. She sipped from her cup and
leaned back in the chair. Always relax when you could.
But inevitably her mind slipped back to the last interview when she'd discussed her medical career. Four
years ago...

She'd been eighteen then, still at school and standing
outwardly calm but inwardly quaking in front of Miss
Jagger's—the headmistress—desk.

Miss Jagger was only just over five feet tall but she
was a dragon. She'd stood, immaculate in her academic
gown and with pure white hair, and stared at Zanne.
Zanne had stared back—chin up, shoulders back, face
resolute. When she'd been fifteen and shooting up to
her present height of five feet eight inches, like so
many shy girls, she'd slouched. Miss Jagger didn't like
girls who slouched. She'd made Zanne walk tall, and
had threatened dire consequences if she ever walked

again in that 'inelegant, ungainly, unladylike fashion'.

'I find this very hard to understand, Suzanne,' Miss Jagger said in the soft tones that indicated great wrath. She was the only person who ever used Zanne's full, formal name.

'We confidently expect you to get four grade A passes. You have worked for the Red Cross; you know what medical work is like. May I say that your teachers and I have had no hesitation in giving you an excellent reference. You were born to be a doctor. And now you are telling me you wish to withdraw your application to study medicine, and you wish to enter nursing instead. Why?'

Zanne forced out a few half-formed sentences about having changed her mind.

'Don't mumble, girl! I admit that of the two careers, medicine and nursing, perhaps nursing ultimately demands more. The sacrifices are greater. And you're making a sacrifice now, aren't you?'

'I just thought I'd like to be a nurse,' Zanne said hopelessly.

'So long as you don't want to be a con man. You're a terrible liar, Suzanne, I'd be failing myself and you if I let you leave this room without knowing why you've changed your mind.'

'Personal reasons?' Zanne suggested, knowing that it would do no good.

Miss Jagger snorted. 'That's the half-baked answer offered by my more stupid girls who are either pregnant, fancy themselves in love or both. I think better of you. Now, why do you wish to give up medicine?'

Zanne sighed. This was a decision that had not been easy, and she didn't want anyone else trying to persuade her. But if Miss Jagger wanted the facts she could have them.

'I've tried to keep things quiet and I want you to do the same. It's my problem. In the summer holidays my mother fell downstairs and her back was injured. We thought there was some hope—but yesterday the consultant said that the paralysis was permanent. When she's discharged my mother will be in a wheelchair for the rest of her life.'

'I'm truly sorry, Suzanne. I didn't know.' Miss Jagger frowned. 'You're an only child, aren't you?'

'And my mother's a widow. We have friends, of course, but no close family.'

'You're saying that you're going to sacrifice your hopes to help your mother?'

Zanne stuck out her jaw defiantly. 'There's no sacrifice; it's just my decision. I can live at home and even bring in a little money. I couldn't if I trained as a doctor.'

'Does your mother know about this choice?'

'My mother has been too ill to bother with my decisions,' Zanne stated flatly.

There was silence for a few moments and then Miss Jagger said, 'Sit down. We'll go over all your circumstances and I'll make a couple of phone calls. Then I'll forward your application for nursing training as a matter of urgency. If you change your mind—if anything alters—you will come and tell me?'

'Just wishing won't change circumstances,' Zanne said sadly, and Miss Jagger nodded.

Once started, however, Zanne thoroughly enjoyed her nurse training. She was physically strong and the work was never too taxing. She liked the studying, which was always directed at the strictly practical. And, above all, she loved the contact with the patients on the ward.

It turned out that her mother adapted to life in a wheelchair quite quickly—she had the same determination as her daughter. Zanne's sacrifice had, perhaps, been unnecessary but she pressed on with her nursing; she'd started it so she would finish it. But always at the back of her mind was the idea that one day she would train to become a doctor.

Now she had the chance. She'd applied to only one medical school, that of the University of the North which was based at her own hospital. And she'd been invited to an interview.

'Miss Ripley?' Miss Hope silently appeared in the doorway. 'Dr Dawkins is back now. Would you like to come through?'

She had a moment's nervousness, quickly shaken off. Zanne stood and walked into the adjoining room.

Dr Dawkins was a round little ball of a man with a happy smile and surprisingly shrewd brown eyes. He bobbed over to greet Zanne, shook her hand, apologised for keeping her waiting and escorted her to a chair at one side of a long table. Then he took his own place at the other side of the table between two other men.

'As you know, I am Admissions Tutor,' he said breezily, 'and the choice of whom to admit is supposed to be mine. But everyone needs help, so I have summoned two colleagues. We require a unanimous decision. All three of us must vote for you. Dr Hurst here is a senior lecturer whom you might have seen on the wards.'

'Yes, I have,' Zanne said hesitantly. For some reason

Charles had insisted that no one in the hospital should know about their relationship. He'd said that he didn't want gossip. Zanne felt that they had nothing to be ashamed of, and she didn't like lying or cheating. She had agreed to the deception only reluctantly. And she wasn't very happy when Charles nodded at her coldly.

'And here we have Dr Neil Calder, who is doing some experimental work with us and will be connected to the orthopaedics department. He's just returned from a long trip abroad.' The third member of the little party stood and reached over the table. 'We meet again, Nurse Ripley,' he acknowledged unsmilingly, and gripped her hand.

He'd changed. Before he'd been pleasant, charming even. Now he was cold and remote. She didn't like it.

He released her hand, and with a slight shock Zanne realised that Dr Dawkins was speaking to her.

'Let's start with an easy question. Will you tell us a little about yourself?'

Zanne had rehearsed her answer to this. The trick was not to be too brief but also not to bore people with a pointless biography. She mentioned her schooling, and how she enjoyed her training as a nurse.

'Have you any hobbies, Miss Ripley? Do you find time for other things apart from nursing?'

This was another well-known trick question. Students who claimed to spend all their time working were seen as bores, not having the well-rounded character that made a good doctor. Zanne said, 'I read a lot and I'm a keen member of the Belham Climbing and Canoeing Club.' She felt, rather than saw, Dr Calder look at her speculatively.

Dr Dawkins asked a couple more questions which

made Zanne realise that behind the amiable face there was a very acute brain. She thought she answered quite well. Then it was Charles's turn. His questions were simply medical ones; Zanne had studied hard and knew that her answers were perfect. Charles nodded at Dr Dawkins, showing that he was satisfied.

There was only Dr Calder left, and for the first time Zanne felt faint unease as he stared at her. He seemed a more formidable figure than the other two. 'Miss Ripley, your A level results were excellent so there's one obvious question. Why didn't you apply to read medicine when you left school?'

Zanne had half expected this question and had decided to answer it honestly. 'I did apply,' she said quietly, and went on to explain about her mother.

Both Charles and Dr Dawkins nodded understandingly. Dr Calder did not. 'And did you find that this decision on your part was really justified?' he asked.

Zanne had expected a little more sympathy but she supposed that it was a fair query. 'I did what I thought best. In fact, my mother coped extremely well and would have built up a life quite without my help. But even if I'd known that I would still have stayed at home with her.'

This time there was a definite encouraging smile from Dr Dawkins. Dr Calder, however, pressed on remorselessly. 'But this means that after four years' nurse training, you will be studying for a further six. Ten years' study before you begin to pay anything back.'

This was too much! Zanne didn't try to disguise the hard edge to her voice as she said, 'The past four years haven't all been study, Dr Calder. I feel I've done quite enough work on the wards to justify the cost of my tuition.'

'You do?' It was the way he asked the question, not the question itself.

Angrily Zanne said, 'What is more, I think nursing experience would be invaluable to me as a doctor. I've seen too many young doctors on the wards who know plenty about medicine but absolutely nothing about overall patient care. Hospital treatment is a partnership between nurse and doctor—not a boss-worker relationship.'

For a moment the two stared at each other, his face grim and expressionless, hers blushing slightly as she realised that perhaps she had allowed her anger to get the better of her judgement.

It was Dr Dawkins who calmed the situation. 'I have to say that in some respects I agree with you, Miss Ripley. But how the BMA would respond to a further long period of study, I don't know. Dr Calder, have you any further questions?'

'Thank you, no; I am quite satisfied.'

'Then I only have to thank you, Miss Ripley, for submitting yourself to this ordeal. I'm sure you know that the demand for places in medical school is very great. But. . .' he beamed at her '. . .you'll get a letter from my office in the next week or two.'

'Thank you, gentlemen,' she said, and walked to the door.

She'd already decided what to do after her interview. It was straight back, get changed and into the hurly-burly of the ward. Only when she and Mary managed to grab a quick drink late in the afternoon did she have a chance to talk and think about what had happened.

'I don't know, Mary. I thought it didn't go too badly. But there was a really awkward customer there—a Dr Neil Calder. Have you heard of him?'

Mary frowned. 'Somebody did tell me something. . . Yes, you should get on with him; he's one of your climbing loonies. Just come back from Everest or something where he's been on a big expedition.'

Something twitched in the back of Zanne's mind, but at that moment a harrassed looking student nurse put her face round the office door and said, 'Sorry, Sister, but Mr Brightman has woken up and he says he can't stand the pain. Can you. . .?' Zanne swiftly walked to the door as Mary moved to the locked cupboard to get the pethidine for an intramuscular injection.

At eight o'clock that evening she was waiting for Charles in the snug of the Kinton Arms. They met there quite regularly; he'd suggested it because it was just far enough away from the hospital that there was little chance of their seeing friends or colleagues there. Zanne saw no good reason why they should try to avoid people they knew, but Charles had insisted.

Now she saw him hurrying towards her, his bright blond hair, carefully parted as ever, shining in the light. 'I've got some good news,' he said as he slumped beside her.

Zanne grasped his hand, her eyes shining. 'I've got the place!' she cried. 'They've accepted me in medical school!'

Charles frowned. 'I said *I've* got some good news.

You won't hear the result of your interview for a while yet.'

Zanne was disappointed. 'But how did I do?'

Charles pursed his lips in the somewhat pompous manner he adopted when talking to the nurses on the ward. 'Well, I can't really tell you. I supported you, of course, but I was only the junior man there, and the other two were still talking when I had to leave.'

'But you thought I didn't do too badly?'

'You upset that bloke Calder. But don't let it worry you. I thought you put up quite a good fight. Now, d'you want to know my good news?'

In fact, Zanne thought that Charles could have been a bit more sympathetic, but he was obviously bubbling with something so she smiled and said, 'Tell me.'

From inside his jacket pocket Charles drew a large envelope and slapped it down on the table. 'It's from the Rentshaw hospital in North London. I've been offered the job of Junior Registrar in Surgery.'

'Charles, that's wonderful!' Impulsively Zanne reached over and kissed him on the cheek; she was pleased for him. 'It's what you've been looking for. When do you start?'

'When I've finished my stint here. I want to get out of this dump and live somewhere civilised.'

Zanne repressed the disloyal thought that 'this dump' had been good enough to train him for the past eight years and said, 'You must be really pleased. But won't you feel sorry at leaving your friends?'

'Zanne, that's what I want to talk to you about. You know what I'm going to say don't you?'

'No,' said Zanne, puzzled.

Charles forced a small laugh. 'You must do. I'm

going to London soon.' He smiled triumphantly. 'I want you to come with me.'

Zanne looked at him in astonishment; she could hardly believe what she was hearing. What was he talking about? She sat silently as various not-very-welcome thoughts whizzed through her brain. Charles took her silence to indicate agreement.

'I'm fed up with living in hospital accommodation. With the two of us earning, there should be no difficulty in renting quite a reasonable flat down there. In fact, I know they're short of nurses—you'll probably end up getting paid more than me at first.' He leaned back, clearly satisfied with his carefully worked out plan.

'You've obviously thought quite a lot about this,' she observed quietly. If Charles had been more perceptive he might have noticed the underlying steel in her voice.

'I have. It seems the best for all concerned.'

'Good.' Zanne stood and flashed a smile at him. 'Have you got any change? I must phone my mother and tell her—she'll be delighted. Then I want to phone Mary because I want her daughters to be bridesmaids.'

Charles froze, open-mouthed, and as the significance of Zanne's words sank in a coin slipped out of his grasp to rattle on the table. 'Bridesmaids?' he croaked.

'I want at least two and a big white wedding. Who will you have as your best man?'

Charles made a valiant effort to recover. 'Zanne, my dear, I think we're at cross-purposes. I wasn't asking you to marry me—just to come to London and to live with me. Perhaps, in time, when we get to know each other better. . .' He shrugged, to indicate that anything might happen. 'But at this stage of my career I can't get tied down.'

'Ah, I see. My mistake. I'm sorry. And what about my going to medical school here?'

'Well, since I'm a doctor I don't see that we need. . .' But one glance at Zanne's iron-hard face made even Charles realise that things weren't going his way. He stammered something about perhaps he'd been a bit premature; perhaps they ought to wait a while before making any decisions—at least until Zanne got the result of her interview.

'I think that would be an excellent idea,' she said. 'And, Charles, to save everybody further embarrassment let me say that I would never live with you, or anybody, until I had a wedding ring on my finger. Is that clear?'

'Perfectly,' said Charles, swallowing. 'Perfectly. Would you like another drink?'

'I think I need one.'

For a week afterwards Zanne was half angry, half amused at Charles. Then a letter came from the admissions tutor of the medical school. There was nothing personal about it, apart from her inked-in name. It was obviously duplicated and even the signature was stamped. It thanked Zanne for her application, pointed out that there were many applicants and few places and said that unfortunately her application had been unsuccessful.

CHAPTER TWO

THE annual dance of the Belham Climbing and Canoeing Club tended to be lively rather than grand. The committee had hired a room at the back of the Belham Hall Hotel, engaged their usual caterers and disco and expected everything to be as much of a success as it usually was.

Zanne was enjoying herself, throwing herself into the throbbing beat of the dance, her long hair for once untied and flowing free in a great black wave to her waist. Her body moved rhythmically, gracefully, as she spun and twisted, her new dress swirling round her knees.

Climbers always seemed to need space for their dancing. They'd picked a room with a suitably sized dance-floor so Zanne could give her enthusiasm full expression. Most people sat above, round candle-lit tables, in a gallery on three sides of the room.

With a final crashing chord, the music came to an end. Derrick Murphy, a local solicitor who was club president, grinned broadly as Zanne turned one final pirouette and sank into a demure curtsey. 'Five minutes dancing with you and I need a drink,' he said. 'You'll wear an old man out. Can I get you anything?'

Zanne shook her head. 'I'm fine for the moment. You get back to your party and I'll say hello to a few people.' Courteously he took her to the edge of the floor before she moved away.

Charles hadn't accompanied her, which was a pity; she would have liked a partner to show off. But he had pleaded pressure of work. Zanne suspected that it had been an excuse; she knew he didn't much like what he called her hairy-chested friends. By unspoken mutual consent they had decided not to mention his proposal about London for a while. Zanne knew that she needed time to think about her future.

When she'd received that dreadful letter she'd phoned Charles at once. She'd thought the admissions tutor had been on her side and she couldn't understand how, with Charles supporting her, she'd been rejected.

'Well, we've been told that every discussion has to be confidential,' Charles had hedged 'and you know we had to be unanimous. But I will say one thing. That fellow Calder is supposed to have a bit of a down on women. Something to do with an incident on this expedition he's just come back from.'

Suddenly Zanne had remembered an article in one of her climbing magazines. There had been an expedition up one of the Himalayan peaks, acknowledged to be tougher than Everest, and it had had to turn back well short of the summit because the only female member of the team had fallen ill.

'He can't blame me for that!' she'd snorted. 'I was applying to be a doctor, not a mountaineer.'

'Calder can do what he likes. He's really shaking things up and everyone's afraid of him. Apparently he's got lots of influential friends.'

'Bully for him.'

'Sorry, Zanne. I really am. Nothing I could do.'

But as Zanne had rung off she'd felt that there had not been conviction in his voice, and she'd wondered how much longer their rather half-hearted affair would last when he finally went to London.

In her doleful frame of mind she'd decided to do something to cheer herself up and so had bought herself this dress which had cost a ridiculous amount of money. It was long, white and lacy and worth every penny. It made her feel like a millionairess. Feeling that she might as well really treat herself, she had also bought matching silk bra and briefs, dainty and frivolous—not at all like the utilitarian underwear she wore for work.

For five minutes she chatted with a group, then accepted another invitation to dance. She was among friends here and knew she'd have no shortage of partners and that she'd have no trouble with any of them.

The evening was passing amiably. After the shortest of speeches there was a break for refreshments and then more dancing. She had an ever-present succession of partners. Above her, on the gallery, she could hear roars of laughter as some of the younger, wilder members played their usual boisterous party games. The management didn't mind; they knew that anything broken would be paid for.

Still, it was getting warm. After a particularly energetic dance she decided to walk outside for a minute, feeling the need for cool air. Carrying her glass of white wine, she stepped out onto the veranda.

The verandah was deserted and when the door shut behind her the rhythmic thud of the disco seemed muffled and distant. There was a hint of spring in the breeze that swept down from the moors above Belham. Happily, she closed her eyes and gave herself to the scents of evening.

The footsteps on the wooden floor were light, and

obviously approaching her. Half irritated at having her moment's vigil interrupted, she didn't turn until the last moment.

The lights were behind the figure in front of her, so that all she could see was a silhouette. It was a male figure and the man was big; he towered inches above her. At first she thought she didn't know who it was, but then there was something about the set of the broad shoulders and the angle of the neck that she vaguely recognised. A faint frisson of anxiety ran down her spine and then the figure stepped into the light of a window.

With a sick realisation she knew who the man was; the breath hissed through her teeth and her anxiety turned into anger. What was Dr Neil Calder doing here?

For a moment the two stood silently, facing each other, then he said, 'Good evening, Nurse Ripley.'

She had intended to flee back to the dance, knowing that she had nothing to say to this man, but since he had spoken first she had to reply. Her mouth was suddenly dry and she sipped her wine before speaking. 'Dr Calder, isn't it? I didn't expect to see you here.' She was proud of her control; her voice sounded remote, indifferent.

He didn't speak for a moment and she felt the anger churning inside her. This man was responsible for her not getting into medical school! Coldly she went on, 'I'm afraid this is a private function. Casual visitors are not allowed in.'

He stepped half a pace forward and, hating herself for doing it, Zanne had to retreat. She didn't want him invading her body space. She could see him more clearly now; like the senior members of the club inside, he was dressed in a dinner jacket. A red rose in his lapel was the only touch of colour in his perfect black and white outfit. As his hand dipped into his pocket, she had a sudden premonition that she'd made a mistake.

His voice sounded amused. 'With you on the door, Nurse Ripley, it would be a brave man who tried to gate-crash. However—' he took a slip of white card from his pocket '—I have a ticket and I am not a casual visitor. I'm the president's guest.'

'You're a bit late for a guest.' The words slipped out before Zanne could stop them.

'That is true,' he agreed, equably. 'And I was looking forward to being here earlier. But just as I was setting out there was a call from young Dave Beck in Casualty. There'd been a car crash and the front seat passenger had broken ribs and a dislocated shoulder. Dave said he could fix it, but if I'd like to look in for five minutes he'd be pleased.' He sighed. 'The five minutes stretched to two and a half hours.'

'That's what happens when you're on call,' she said unfeelingly.

'I know it does. But I wasn't on call.'

Zanne decided that the conversation had gone on long enough. 'Derrick Murphy's the president,' she said abruptly. 'He's just inside. I'll take you to him. He'll be wondering where you are.'

As she turned to the door he grasped her gently by the arm. Zanne stood rigid at his touch; she couldn't move. What's happening to me? she asked herself, aghast. His fingers could not have been lighter on her skin and yet she knew that she could more easily break iron chains than shake off his hand. It was only seconds, yet it seemed like an eternity, before he let her go and she glanced down at her arm, expecting to see the mark of his fingers blazoned there.

'He won't be wondering; I sent a message saying I'd be late,' Dr Calder said softly. 'Now, I've been busy all afternoon and then all evening. I've raced over here because I don't like breaking arrangements. What would be really pleasant is to stay here for five minutes just to get my breath back and to enjoy the evening air.'

'I'll fetch you a drink,' she offered, desperate to get away.

'I don't need a drink. I need some peace.'

'Don't we all?' she asked bitterly. 'How did you remember my name?'

He glanced at her assessingly. 'I had no difficulty in remembering you or your name. You made quite an impact in your interview.'

'Not enough impact for you to offer me a place,' she said bitingly. For a moment she thought he looked slightly abashed so she went on, 'Don't worry, Dr Calder, I'm not going to ask you to betray medical secrecy. The decision is made; I don't need explanations. Tell me, are you a personal friend of Derrick Murphy?'

The sudden change in the topic of conversation didn't seem to surprise him. 'I've never met him before, but we have mutual friends. He wrote to me asking if I would give a talk to the club on my last expedition.'

That was it! It made sense now. Sweetly Zanne said, 'I'll look forward to it. Will you be talking about the undesirability of women on Himalayan expeditions?'

She had to admit that he took it well. He sighed and said in a resigned voice, 'I think I will go inside; there might be more peace there. To answer your question,

Miss Ripley, if I'm asked I shall say that the strongest, best trained, most experienced male mountaineers will usually outclimb the strongest, best trained, most experienced female mountaineers. It's a function of the basic differences between the two sexes. Good evening.'

There was a brief swell of sound as he pulled open the door and then peace again as he closed it behind him, and Zanne was left alone. Her mind was in a turmoil. Neil Calder wasn't what she'd expected.

Certainly he was arrogant—well, assured of his own competence—but she thought she'd detected a slight touch of humanity somewhere. He must work hard to hide it, she decided, and forced herself not to think of what had happened when he had touched her. For a moment something electric had passed between them. It was a feeling she'd had with no other man. She shrugged and walked back into the dance. She was imagining things.

The party was now going with a real swing. Breathlessly Zanne enjoyed dance after dance, swinging, swaying, arms above her head, as she moved to the insistent beat.

In a quiet moment she looked round the room but could see neither Derrick Murphy nor Dr Calder. Then after twenty minutes they appeared together on the gallery; obviously they'd been having a quieter drink in the hotel bar.

Perhaps Dr Calder felt her gaze; he glanced down to see her staring at him. She flushed as she realised he knew she'd been looking at him and deliberately flashed her partner a brilliant, if slightly forced, smile.

I wish that man hadn't come, she thought to herself; he's disturbing me.

The temperature had risen again and at the end of the dance there was a chorus of screams and shouts of approval from the gallery. Looking up, she saw Peter Collins, one of the younger members, walking with arms outstretched along the bannister. Situation normal—for Peter's set no party was complete without some kind of athletic or balancing feat. She grinned and decided to go to the cloakroom to freshen up.

Dabbing gently at her face with the tissues provided by the management, she wondered if she'd go to Dr Calder's talk—if he gave one, that was. On reflection, she thought probably not. The man only angered her. In fact, she was angry that she seemed to be spending so much time thinking about him. It wasn't what he'd done to her. It was. . . She gave up.

There was no one else in the cloakroom but Zanne's brow suddenly crinkled. Something nudged the edge of her consciousness. That was it; it was a change in sound—the background buzz of the party had altered radically in tone. Zanne picked up overtones of anxiety, even fear. Something was wrong. Hastily she went back to the dance.

Someone had turned on all the lights; instead of the dim, intimate atmosphere there was a harsh glare reflecting concern on every face. People were standing craning their necks, and just under the overhanging gallery a tight knot of dark-suited figures was crowded round someone on the floor. Zanne hurried over.

'It's Peter,' an ashen-faced friend told her. 'He fell off the gallery. His foot caught and he bashed into the floor head first.'

Zanne winced, then pushed at the two backs nearest her. 'I'm a nurse; let me through,' she snapped and obediently a way was made for her.

Peter had fallen hard. He was lying on his back, unconscious. Kneeling just behind him was Dr Calder, one hand cradling Peter's neck and the other easing his jaw back. He looked up as Zanne burst through the crowd.

'Suspected cervical fracture, Nurse,' he said curtly. 'I've felt; there's a slight step—I think it's C7. I daren't let go.'

Zanne understood at once. Any sudden movement and the spinal cord could be bruised, even cut. That could mean paralysis or even death.

'Who's phoned for an ambulance?' she asked loudly. It was amazing how, in a situation like this, everyone imagined that someone else would do it.

People looked at each other guiltily and Zanne pointed at an older man. 'Colin, you go and do it now.' She turned to the tense figure behind Peter's head. 'Have you any instructions, Dr Calder?'

Dark eyes flicked her way. 'I haven't been able to make any kind of examination. His hips crashed into a table on the way down and I heard glass breaking. Can you check—? Quickly, find where that blood's coming from!' Both saw it at the same time—the dark stain of blood on Peter's thigh, growing larger even as they looked.

Zanne started to stoop—and could have cried. Her dress, so wonderful for dancing, wasn't designed for impromptu nursing. If she was going to kneel she'd have to tear it. There was only one thing to do.

Turning to the nearest man she said, 'Quick, unzip

me.' He did, and a second later she felt the back of her dress come apart. Zanne leaned forward, shook off the shoulders, then pushed the white material over her hips and stepped out of the dress. Might as well do the job properly, she thought to herself, and kicked off her moderately high heels. Then, clad solely in bra and briefs, she knelt and unfastened Peter's belt.

Peter had smashed into a glass as he fell, and there was a long cut across his abdomen which deepened as it led onto his thigh. There was a lot of blood and she saw the glint of a fragment still in the wound. Carefully she eased it out. 'Get me some clean napkins,' she ordered, and someone handed her a bunch. When she wiped away the rapidly pooling blood she saw what she'd feared—the regular pulse that indicated arterial bleeding.

'I think the femoral artery is cut,' she said to Dr Calder.

'From here it looks as if it's only nicked. Get a pressure pad on it now.' The doctor looked up. 'Will all of you with clean handkerchiefs give them to the nurse?'

Quickly she seized the white squares that fluttered onto Peter's chest, wadded them into a pad and pressed it with all her weight onto the source of the spurting blood. It seemed to be successful; the flow diminished. She nodded her satisfaction to Dr Calder. 'All right for now.'

'Then we wait.' Once again he looked up. 'Will a couple of you go to the front of the hotel and guide the ambulancemen here? Tell them to bring a hard collar.'

As two men ran off Zanne heard Derrick Murphy

speak. 'Is there anything we can do? We all feel helpless.'

'For the moment everything's under control,' the doctor said tersely. 'We wait and we hope.' Zanne flexed her arms slightly to ease her now cramped shoulders and did as he recommended.

It didn't seem long before there came the distant, familiar wail of the ambulance siren, shortly followed by uniformed men placing a stretcher beside Peter's body. Zanne knew that these men were better trained than she to deal with emergencies, so she happily allowed one to take her place and expertly place a compress and strap over the wound. Dr Calder was easing Peter's neck into the hard collar that would immobilise it. Then the stretcher was wheeled out.

Zanne stood up wearily. There was blood staining her hands and her thighs and splashed across her chest. It hadn't worried her so far but suddenly she was embarrassed, aware that she was half-naked in a room full of people. As if he guessed her thoughts Dr Calder took off his jacket and wrapped it round her.

'Congratulations, Nurse,' he said. 'You did very well there.'

'But not well enough to be a doctor?'

A flicker of grudging amusement passed over his face, but he didn't answer her question. 'You're in a bit of a mess,' he said in a matter-of-fact tone. 'Perhaps you'd better go and clean up.'

Zanne walked back to the cloakroom.

She washed off what she could but her new underwear was stained and there was no way that she was going to put on her dress again. With casual thoughtfulness one of the girls brought her in a cup of sweet tea, another lent her a tracksuit and trainers and a third carefully folded and packed her dress. Zanne dispatched one with Dr Calder's jacket; she returned to say that the doctor had gone back to the hospital.

'He's quite something, that Dr Calder, isn't he, Zanne? We all were really fancying him. D'you know him well?'

'I've met him a couple of times,' Zanne said, pretending to be preoccupied. 'He's not really my type.'

'Get on with you! He's every girl's type. If you don't want him bring him here for me.' Zanne sighed. This was a conversation she could do without.

When she left the cloakroom the dance seemed to be starting again, although rather shakily. The disco was playing quietly and groups were forming round the tables again. A couple of Peter's friends had gone to the hospital casualty department and promised to phone if there was any news.

Derrick Murphy walked over to Zanne. 'I want to thank you, Zanne; you turned what could have been a tragedy into just an accident.'

She shrugged. 'Dr Calder did more than me, Derrick. It was all in a day's work.'

'Not the kind of work I could do, nor anyone else here. Now, d'you want a drink?'

She shook her head. 'I think I'll call it a day. It's been a great party—at least up till Peter falling—but I've had enough.'

'Fair enough,' he nodded. 'Now, this time there'll be no argument. I'm running you home.'

'But, Derrick. . .'

'I said, no argument. It's only ten minutes away.'
Zanne decided that she felt too deflated to argue.

In fact, she got Derrick to drop her off at the hospital.
She went to Casualty first, where she heard that Dr
Calder had called in but had then gone home. She'd
have to return his jacket on Monday. Peter was in
Theatre; unofficially she was told that things were
serious but not dangerous. She passed this on to his
two gloomy-looking friends waiting outside and
decided not to stay with them.

What now? She knew that there would be no point
in walking the half-mile to her home—she'd never rest.
Aimlessly she went to the nurses' common-room and
poured herself a coffee.

There was no one to talk to. She flipped through a
couple of magazines and then, almost in desperation,
turned to see if there was anything new on the
noticeboard. There were the usual offers of accommodation, services with reductions for nurses and
handwritten notes of articles for sale. And there was
something else—something new:

> Wanted for five months over summer. Resident
> staff nurse for mountain activities centre in the Lake
> District. Ideally applicants should have some know-
> ledge of camping/walking/climbing/canoeing. Those
> interested should phone. . .

She read the short notice through three times. Up to
this week her future had been planned: she'd intended
to go to medical school in September. But that chance
had now gone. Her mother was getting married, then

going to Canada for an indefinite stay. Zanne loved her work on the ward but. . .

She scribbled down the telephone number.

CHAPTER THREE

ZANNE didn't sleep well that night and woke early on Sunday morning, irritable and unable to decide why she was so dissatisfied with life. She banged about the kitchen, working out her ill-temper by doing her handwashing and the small jobs that had accumulated during the week. Eventually her mother sought refuge with the papers in the lounge.

It's not just being rejected for medical training, she told herself as she scrubbed viciously at her blood-stained bra; it's that I'm. . . But she didn't know what was wrong, and this made her angrier than ever. Images of Dr Neil Calder kept floating across her mind and she wondered what he was really like.

At lunchtime there was a surprise. A sheaf of flowers was delivered—red, yellow and white roses surrounded by maidenhair fern. There was an accompanying note from Derrick Murphy, thanking her on behalf of the committee for what she had done for young Peter and saying that he'd been in touch with the hospital and Peter was now well out of danger.

'It's nice to get thanks,' her mother said, busily arranging the flowers in her best cut-glass vase. 'Just what did you do to deserve them?'

'Oh, nothing much. One of the lads fell and cut his leg,' Zanne said, being deliberately vague. When her mother had first been getting used to living in her wheelchair Zanne had decided on a definite policy of never talking too much about troubles on the wards. She felt that her mother had enough to cope with her own problems without being subjected to other people's.

Her mother looked at her with some irritation. 'It's an expensive bunch of flowers for nothing much,' she said. 'I'm a big girl now, Zanne; you can tell me things.' A surprisingly youthful smile spread across her face. 'Don't forget I'll soon be a married woman.'

'So you will be. Deserting me! You're off gadding to Canada with a young man while I toil here at my humble job.'

'Quite so. I'm striking a blow for grey wheelchair power. Now. . .these look quite lovely.' Elizabeth placed the flowers on the sideboard and then abruptly wheeled round to face her daughter. 'How many years have you lived in this house, Zanne?'

She looked up, surprised at her mother's serious tone. 'You know very well—all my life. I've been here twenty-two years and I love it.'

'You went to a school only a mile away and now you work at a hospital that is even closer.'

'Both very convenient,' Zanne said uneasily. She didn't like the way her mother's words were so close to thoughts she'd had herself.

'I'm going to Canada for six months at least, and when I get back I shall move into Joe's bungalow with him. There's a home there for you if you want it, or you certainly can live here. But isn't it about time you had a change?'

'I don't know; perhaps it is,' Zanne said fretfully. 'But I don't want to think about it now. Can we talk about something else?'

'Of course,' said Elizabeth, hiding a smile. She had suspected what her daughter was thinking, and had decided to give things a push in the right direction. Zanne, however, was more restless than ever. From her pocket she took out the telephone number she had copied out the night before and looked at it broodingly. Then she put it on her bedroom mantelpiece.

At lunchtime Charles rang; she took the call on her bedside phone. He did remember to ask her if she'd enjoyed herself at the dance last night, but it was obvious that he had other, more important things to say to her.

'I've been invited down to London next weekend to have a look round the department and I was wondering if you'd like to come with me. We could do a bit of flat-hunting while we were there.'

'Flat-hunting for you or for both of us?'

'Well, for both of us, of course. I know you were disappointed at not getting into medical school, but I thought you'd have got over it by now.'

'And am I supposed to get over my objections to living with someone without being married?'

'Zanne,' the long-suffering voice on the telephone sighed, 'this is the late twentieth century. It's just not necessary to get married any more. Look around you.'

For a moment she was tempted—just a little. She'd get a complete change of scene; there would be the chance to nurse in a different environment, and Charles could be quite good company. But even as the thoughts flitted across her mind she knew what her answer would be. It was almost with a feeling of relief that she said, 'Sorry, Charles. I'm just not interested.'

He obviously heard the certainty in her voice because

he said angrily, 'Do you realise what that means? I shall be very busy in my new post. It's going to be very demanding—I certainly shan't have time to travel up here just to see you.'

With deadly calm she said, 'No, Charles, you won't have time to travel up here just to see me. You won't have any need either. I'll make this neat, clean and easy. Charles, it's all over between us. Goodbye.'

As ever, Charles managed to say completely the wrong thing. He spluttered, 'Zanne, you can't do this. I want you to—'

She cut in. 'Wrong on both counts. I can do it and what you want no longer matters. I said goodbye.' Then she rang off.

For five minutes she sat on her bed, gloomily waiting for him to ring back. When he didn't she began to relax a little. She knew that she'd done the right thing. But, still, she'd been seeing him for a while and they'd had some good times together. As she tried to recapture them she realised that the times hadn't been all that good, and she'd always subconsciously thought him a bore. This realisation made her more angry than ever.

She'd moped long enough! Quickly she pulled on her old grey tracksuit, crammed her feet into trainers and roughly tied her hair back. After shouting an explanation to her mother, she dashed out of the front door and cut through the alley opposite which led to the park.

Once through the gates she jogged up the long, grassy stretch that led to the park's running track. There she jumped up and down for a few moments to make sure that she was adequately warmed up. Then it was onto the hard springy surface, heart beating and pulse racing, lap after lap—the sheer strain and joy of exercise driving out the irritations and doubts that seemed to be plaguing her.

Half an hour later she was nearly exhausted but life was good again. She trotted down the hill and then sprinted the last half-mile home to burst through the front door, feeling considerably better than when she'd left. She pulled off her hair band so that her luxuriant black hair swept down over her shoulders. Breathing deeply, her face flushed with exertion, she shouted, 'I'm back, Ma,' and walked in to the living-room.

'Hello, dear,' her mother smiled as Zanne entered. 'Here's Dr Calder come to see you.'

At that moment there was a short beep from a car's horn outside. 'That must be Joe,' her mother said. 'I told him not to come to the door.' She wheeled her way past Zanne, who was too shocked to move. 'I'll be back at about six, Zanne, and Joe's coming to tea.' She winked at her flabbergasted daughter and then turned. 'So nice to meet you, Doctor. I do hope we meet again.'

'I hope so, too.' The door closed softly behind Zanne and she was left alone with Dr Neil Calder.

He had risen to his feet as Zanne entered the room and the two eyed each other speechlessly. Her first, irrelevant thought was that he always looked well whatever he was wearing. She had seen him in a well-cut suit and dark tie at the hospital, an equally sombre dinner jacket, and now he was wearing casual trousers with a burgundy polo-necked sweater and a light grey leather coat. He still looked well.

He spoke first. 'Your mother made some tea. Why

don't you sit down and have a cup with me? You look as if you need a rest.'

'No,' she gasped. She felt defenceless. It struck her that he looked like something out of the men's section of *Vogue*, while she was hot, sweaty and dishevelled. 'I'll go and have a shower. I must look a mess.'

'You look magnificent,' he said quietly, and she shivered as something in his gaze told her that he meant it. He reached over and grasped her wrist. 'But you're warm and your pulse is fast. You know very well that you need to rest before you shower.'

She heard what he was saying and vaguely she recognised that it was true. It took an effort to pull her arm away, but she did it and said hesitantly, 'I need to change.' She indicated the well-worn tracksuit and the cascade of hair. 'I don't usually receive guests dressed this way.' What she meant was that she needed time to get over the shock of seeing him, tall and urbane, in her mother's living-room.

'Rubbish. Sit down and I'll pour the tea—your mother left a cup ready for you.'

'All right.' Unable to think of anything more to say, she collapsed into a chair—the one furthest from him. There was silence for a moment and she noticed that his actions as he collected cup and teapot were deft and assured, the movements of a fit, trained athlete.

He offered her her tea. 'And as for seeing you dressed like that—' he smiled '—I've seen you in a suit, in nurse's uniform, evening dress and, lastly, hardly anything at all.'

She blushed at the memory and said defensively, 'I paid a lot for that dress and it seemed a good idea at the time. I just wasn't thinking.'

'I disagree. You could have left the lad alone, or torn your dress and still made a mess of treating the bleeding. Instead, you came up with a perfect example of lateral thinking. You took the dress off.'

'And appeared nearly naked in the middle of a dance-floor.'

He shook his head. 'It wasn't like that. I looked round and I couldn't see a single man looking at you in any prurient way. You were among friends, Zanne, who were grateful for what you were doing.'

'I suppose so.' She was getting her breath and her composure back now. Why should she be embarrassed at the presence of this man? She was in her own house and he had come uninvited. What's more, he was the one who had stopped her getting to medical school; the man who apparently thought that women were all right as nurses but not as doctors.

'I suppose you've come for your coat,' she said abruptly, and saw his eyes flicker; obviously he'd registered her change of tone. However, when he replied there was no indication of his feelings.

'I heard you were looking for me last night, but I'd left.'

'There was no need to call here for it. I would happily have brought it to you tomorrow.'

'I'm sure you would but I'm afraid I have to pack it tonight. I have to go on leave a week earlier than planned. Tomorrow I'm flying over to Geneva for a conference on medicine at high altitude and I'm giving a paper. Then I'm going to a mountaineering school in Chamonix to finish some experiments. I might get some climbing in, too.'

'How nice,' she said frostily. 'A conference, climbing and a chance to wear your dinner jacket.'

'You mean it's all right for some and why couldn't it be you?'

She blushed and then saw the humour swirling in those deep grey eyes and reluctantly had to laugh with him. He had guessed her thoughts almost exactly. 'I'm just a bit jealous,' she said. 'I've never been to France and I've always fancied it.'

'Never? It's not too far away.'

She shrugged. 'I've only been abroad twice; each time I went for a week to Benidorm with my friends from the ward. They all thought I was mad; I went walking in the mountains behind the town while they sunned themselves on the beach all day.' After a pause she went on, 'I guess you're entitled to your stay in Geneva, I'm sure you worked for it.'

'I like to think so.'

There was a pause for a moment and Zanne wondered exactly what was happening. She hated this man—he'd turned her down for medical school. But when they were alone together she had to admit that he was good company. How could this cheerful person, sprawled in a chair opposite her, be the cold-eyed doctor who had rejected her? She would have to be careful; he could so easily change again.

He'd been looking round the room in which they were sitting, a slightly abstracted expression on his face. 'I had a chat with your mother before you came,' he said. 'She's a very nice lady. You know, after five minutes talking to her you forget she's in a wheelchair.' He looked round again. 'I can see how this room's organised to suit her—but it's still a very pleasant place to sit.'

'She's very independent,' Zanne said. 'That's one reason I wanted to stay with her—I knew she wouldn't ask for the help that I could give, whether she wanted me to or not.'

He nodded. 'She's got a lot to be grateful to you for.'

'She has not,' Zanne snapped. 'I did nothing more than any daughter would do.'

'Or any son would do?'

That really angered her and she opened her mouth to say something cutting and unpleasant. Then she noticed a slight air of tension in the otherwise relaxed figure and realised that the question had not been lightly put. He was testing her.

Carefully, she said, 'I realise that it's always been seen as the woman's job to stay at home and look after any parent who needed it, but I think things are starting to change now. More sons are spending time with their parents. Just as more women are becoming doctors.'

'Change always comes slowly,' he said, but she felt that he sympathised with what she had said.

She noticed that he'd finished his tea and realised what he'd just told her. He was flying abroad the next day and she knew he was a busy man. He'd come for his jacket and he'd been kept waiting for nearly an hour. Rising to her feet, she said, 'I've been chattering here while you must have a lot to do. I'll get your jacket now.'

He didn't speak but merely inclined his head. Zanne fetched the jacket from the cupboard under the stairs. She handed it to him, then said in some confusion, 'I'm sorry; let me wrap it in something. It looks a bit— well, naked like that.'

He shook his head. 'Nonsense. I've got a hanger in

the back of the car—it will do very well there.'

'And thank you for lending it to me,' she added.

'It was my pleasure.' He took the jacket and then, with a mischievous expression, held it to his nose. 'Chanel No. 5,' he said with evident satisfaction.

Zanne was mortified. 'You can smell my talcum powder! I'm sorry. Here, I'll have it dry-cleaned; I didn't realise. . .'

'You'll do no such thing. I like it,' he said flatly. 'I'm sorry, it was rude of me to comment.' For a moment he stood abstractedly, then said, ' "It smells. . .not of itself, but thee." '

'I beg your pardon?' she said, by now thoroughly confused.

'It's a poem I like by Ben Jonson. Now, I really must go. Please thank your mother for the tea. And thank you, Nurse, for what you did yesterday. Perhaps I'll see you when I return from France?'

'I'll try to get there when you give your talk to the club,' she said deliberately.

'Goodbye till then.' And he was gone. She heard an obviously expensive engine start in the street outside and, shaken, closed the door.

This was too much. She'd been irritated, out of sorts and restless that morning; her run had largely calmed her. And then Neil Calder had arrived and she was completely on edge again. Why? she asked herself. Because I hate the man? She wasn't certain.

Perhaps a bath would relax her, she thought, turning on both taps. As a treat she threw in two capsules of expensive bath oil, kicked off her tracksuit and then lowered herself into the foaming, scented water. It was blissful. She settled back and waited for peace to come to her churning thoughts. It didn't work. For five minutes she lay there and then climbed out and wrapped a towel round herself.

The scrap of paper with the number was still on her mantelpiece. She sat on the bed and dialled. 'Lawiston Hall Mountain Centre,' a pleasant voice said.

Apparently she needed to talk to John Brownlees, the director. She was lucky that he was in. When he came to the phone Zanne said quickly, 'My name's Zanne Ripley and I'm interested in the nurse's post. I'm an RGN and I've got my Mountain Leadership Certificate.' She was also wet through, getting rather cold and wondering if this was a good idea.

'That's quick work,' the man said. 'The notice was only posted two days ago. Could you tell me a little more about yourself?'

She told him about her hospital work and her membership of the climbing and canoeing club, said that she could probably start quite quickly and that she could get references.

'Why don't you come and have a look round?' John suggested. 'Not an interview—just to see if you like the place.'

She could take next Thursday off; he arranged to pick her up in Ambleside. She returned to her bath.

The water was still warm and this time she would relax. Somehow she'd taken a positive step; her future might now be different. She felt considerably better.

Ambleside was only sixty miles from her home town so Zanne took the bus. Since she was not officially being interviewed she decided not to wear an interview dress. Instead she wore walking boots, trousers and one of her thicker anoraks.

John Brownlees was waiting for her at the bus station. She liked him at once. He was a cheerfully smiling blond man, dressed much like herself and aged about fifty. 'Good to see you, Zanne,' he said, wringing her hand, 'and good to see you dressed for the part.' He looked at her with approval.

'I hope I haven't brought you away from your work?' she ventured as she climbed into the battered Land Rover with LAWISTON HALL MOUNTAIN CENTRE on its side.

He shook his head and pointed to a package on the dashboard. 'I needed to call in. Just had my boots resoled. Now, we'll be there in half an hour. . .'

They took the twisting back roads out of Ambleside and, as ever, she responded to the delicate beauty of early spring. It was colder here than at home but the thin sun shone on the fresh buds and she was contented.

John was an entertaining companion, keeping up a constant flow of conversation. It was only after a while that Zanne realised that she was being interviewed in a most subtle fashion. John had obtained details of her training, her interests and her attitude to work without ever asking her a direct question. She smiled to herself; she liked it.

They turned off the road and stopped by a chained gate leading into a path through the dark conifers that indicated forestry commission land. John climbed out to unlock the gate. 'A short cut,' he said. 'Quite a pleasant one, too.' They bumped through, he relocked the gate and they drove into the long aisle of trees.

It seemed as if she had passed the first test. John no

longer pressed gracefully worded questions on her, but instead told her something of the centre.

'Basically we run three kinds of course. Firstly, we have people who want a holiday but who want to do something on it. We've got experts in literature, history, geology, arts and crafts. You name it, we can run a course on it. We get a lot of people from abroad and they tend to be—well, oldish.

'Then we run courses for managers from industry.' John grinned. 'They're very competitive and need to be reminded that they're not as young as they once were. And, finally, we run an Outward Bound type course for young people. They're trainees, usually sent by companies. All of these occasionally need medical care of some kind.'

'Sounds interesting,' Zanne said. It was a totally different kind of nursing from the intensive, ward-based work she was used to. She rather fancied trying it— not for ever but for a while.

They drove along the forest ride for perhaps two miles. Then the pine trees thinned and they turned off across a cattle-grid. 'We're now in the grounds of Lawiston Hall,' John said. 'We own quite a bit of land.'

It was attractive country, traditional English parkland with copses and great single trees. The rough road dipped, passed a rock face that she realised was climb-able, and a 'rope-garden'—a sort of assault course. She'd been on one before. Then she saw a set of wooden chalets scattered on the valley floor.

'We keep the young people separate from the older ones,' John explained. 'Their course is very intensive so we don't want them distracted. If you like, we'll have lunch down here.'

They ate in a rustic canteen, collecting their food on trays from a serving hatch. Like John, Zanne ate a cheese and egg salad. At first there weren't many people about and Zanne presumed that most were off on exercises. Then a group of five youths clattered into the room and, from various comments that Zanne could hear, they seemed to be less than pleased.

Two minutes later someone crashed his tray onto the table next to her and she looked up to see a large young man in a checked shirt and with his hair in a ponytail. 'Mind if I join you, John?' the man asked. 'And who's this lovely lady?'

John introduced Mike Deeley, one of the resident instructors, and explained that Zanne was looking round the place. She looked at Mike with a slightly jaundiced eye. She didn't mind being described as a lovely lady but there was much more to her than that.

'Why are you back so early?' John was querying. 'I've got you down for a full day's mapwork and orienteering.'

Mike looked up from the vast pile of chips he was demolishing. 'Trouble in the group. Young Nancy's been great so far—only girl with five lads and she's done well. Today she's thrown a wobbler: can't do anything; doesn't feel like walking; doesn't want anything to eat. Says, no, there's nothing wrong with her, but she couldn't keep up so I decided to bring them all home. Women!' Mike was obviously disappointed in Nancy.

'Did you ask her if she was starting her period?' Zanne asked coldly.

It wasn't the reaction Mike had expected. He stared at Zanne, embarrassed and horror-struck, fork held halfway to his mouth. 'No,' he mumbled, 'but she could have told me.'

Zanne jerked her thumb at the cheerfully noisy gang of lads behind her. 'In front of that lot?' she asked.

'I suppose not,' he said and then, with the air of someone who has made a discovery, 'Women are different from men.'

'So they are,' she agreed sweetly. 'Women survive more readily at birth, mature earlier, are more resistant to disease and pain, go senile later and live longer.'

John, trying to hide a grin, said, 'Mike, I should have told you that Zanne is a nurse. She's interested in working with us.'

'What a good idea,' said the irrepressible Mike. 'We certainly need one.'

'Obviously,' Zanne said drily. 'Would you like me to have a word with the girl?'

After lunch Mike took Zanne to the dormitory where he said Nancy was resting. 'I'll see her on my own,' Zanne said. 'You can wait for me out here.'

'Whatever you say, Doc.' She gritted her teeth but Mike wasn't to know that calling her Doc, even in jest, was not the way to ingratiate himself.

Nancy was lying on her bunk, fully clothed, with her arms clutched round her middle. Zanne knew at once that her provisional diagnosis had been right. 'I'm a nurse, Nancy,' she said cheerfully, 'and you've got bad period pains.'

'They've never been this bad before,' the girl gasped, 'and I didn't want to let Mike and the lads down.'

'Don't worry about it. Now, let's have a look at you.'

Showing some initiative, Mike had gone to get the

keys from John and when she came out he took her to the little surgery. She searched through the cupboards and took out the Ponstan. With a hot-water bottle it should do the trick.

'I'll dose her with this,' she told Mike as they went back to the dormitory. 'Let her rest for today and with any luck she'll be fit tomorrow.' She thought a moment and decided that Mike needed the lesson driven firmly home. 'You do carry a first-aid kit when you're on the moors?'

He nodded. 'Of course. All the instructors carry a kit.'

'Good. Are there any spare sanitary towels in it in case of an emergency?'

She had to hide her smile as he croaked, 'Well, no, I don't think so.'

Reprovingly she said, 'It's always a good idea, you know. Unexpected exertion can alter the menstrual cycle quite radically.'

She reassured Nancy and dosed her, and then came out to Mike. She guessed that he was quite happy to hand her back to John.

With John she went back for a longer look round the surgery. It was situated in a chalet on its own, halfway between the main hall and the trainees' centre. There was a treatment room, an office and two small four-bed wards.

'This is not a hospital,' John explained. 'Anything at all serious and off the patient goes. But we don't like to impose on the local health service too much. Mostly we deal with strains, sprains, cuts, bruises and even the occasional bout of sunstroke—though we do

warn people against it. I think a lot of the job is
counselling, too.'

He opened a door at the end of the corridor and
showed Zanne the nurse's own accommodation: a tiny
sitting-room, an even tinier bedroom, bathroom and
kitchen. 'The nurse—actually, we call her Sister—
usually eats with us in the main hall, but this is for
when she wants to be alone.'

'I think it looks ideal,' Zanne said sincerely.

Then they drove up to the main hall. It was a graceful
grey stone building, fitting well into its setting. She
guessed that it dated back to the eighteenth century.
However, when she stepped inside she realised that it
had been efficiently and tastefully modernised.

John took her to his study. 'We get on well with the
local practice,' he said in answer to one of her questions. 'In fact, Dr Alan Mitchell was quite a climber
himself in his younger days. On occasion, when they're
busy or the weather is bad, he or the district nurse ask
us to look in on a local to change dressings or something. We try to pull together.'

He sat her in front of his desk and said, 'Now we
get formal. Does the work interest you, Zanne?'

'Very much so,' she said promptly. 'If there's an
application form I'd like to fill it in. If there isn't I've
already written out a letter of application and filled in
a C.V. Here.' She handed him an envelope.

'Now that,' he said reverently, 'is efficient.'

He read through the two documents and then handed
a paper to her. 'Those are the conditions of service.
We know the money isn't very good, but you do get
board and lodging. We also pride ourselves that the
staff learn here as well as everyone else. After a few

months you'll be a better nurse. We also like to think you'll be a better person.'

He paused for a moment and then went on, 'Would you mind if I telephoned your referees as well as writing to them?'

'I wouldn't mind at all,' she said positively.

'You also realise that this can only be a short contract? Our present sister is taking maternity leave, and swears she'll be back.'

'I realise that.'

There was a tap on the door and they turned to see Mike peering round it. 'Just driven up. Sorry to disturb you again but if there's free medical advice going I'd like some more.'

John grinned and looked at Zanne enquiringly. She said, 'I'd be happy to do what I can.'

'There's a lad just come in from a run, limping badly. When I looked at his foot it seemed to me that he'd had a blister, burst it and it's gone septic.'

'The lads do that,' John said mournfully. 'They don't like to give up.'

'If you've got the keys we'll go back to the surgery.' Zanne said. 'Can you bring him along, Mike?'

She opened the surgery again and Mike soon reappeared with an embarrassed young giant called Martin hobbling behind him. When she examined the foot she saw that Mike had been right—there was an angry red weal on the lad's toes where his boot had obviously been chafing.

'Another day or so and you would have had blood-poisoning,' she remarked. 'It's not tough to ignore things like this—it's foolish.' She winked at him to take the sting out of her words. Deftly she cleaned and dressed the wound and then said, 'Let's see the other foot.'

'It's all right, Nurse,' Martin said placatingly, 'I feel fine now—'

'I said, "the other foot"!'

Looking alarmed, Martin stripped off boot and sock. She pressed a slight inflammation on the side of one heel and noticed his quick intake of breath. 'You'll have another blister there soon, and then you'll be incapable of walking. Now, what you're to do is. . .' She gave him a set of dressings and instructions on how to apply them. Martin walked off looking quite relieved. Zanne smiled to herself. In her climbing club she'd had to deal with dozens of young lads like Martin.

As they returned to John's office she told Mike what she had done, and how he was to check that Martin dressed his feet as she'd told him.

Mike looked at her with some respect. 'I'll see he does that,' he promised.

In the office John was just putting down the phone as they entered. As ever, Mike obviously wanted to stay but John beamed and said, 'I'll see you later, then, Mike,' and he had to take the hint.

'Everything under control?' John asked and she gave a quick report on what she'd done.

'Good.' Formally he said, 'Miss Ripley, I've just phoned both your referees. Based on their recommendations, I should now like to offer you the post of resident sister at the Lawiston Hall Mountain Centre.'

'I accept,' she said at once.

CHAPTER FOUR

SINCE she was going, she might as well go quickly. Zanne handed in a month's notice at the hospital, and then asked for the two weeks' holiday she was owed.

She was surprised and rather gratified at the stir her leaving caused. Obviously her friends would miss her, but senior staff, doctors and consultants all seemed sorry to see her go. One or two tried very hard to persuade her to stay.

'You know I'm getting married next month,' Mary Kelly wailed. 'How can I get married without you to hold my hand?'

'I'm not going far, and nothing will stop me coming back to be your maid of honour.'

And she went. She explained that she'd been in the same place too long; she was getting stale; she needed a change, even though she knew that she'd miss Ward 17. She didn't mention that she'd been turned down for medical training.

The time passed quickly. Only a fortnight on the ward in a whirl of parties and goodbyes and she was ready to go.

Her mother's wedding was a quiet but joyful affair. The honeymoon couple left for Canada. As Zanne waved goodbye at the airport she felt a slight touch of desolation. For the first time in her life she was alone. Then she smiled grimly. Her future was an empty open book. She could write in it what she liked.

Her spare belongings were stored at Joe's—now her stepfather. The bungalow where she'd spent most of her life was let to a visiting doctor and his family. Zanne was ready to go.

A week after she'd accepted the new job there had been a postcard from France—a glorious view of snow-capped peaks. She'd turned it over and seen the bold, clear signature—Neil Calder. Angrily she'd torn the card in half, folded it and torn it again. Then she'd thrown the fragments into her waste-paper basket. That man had turned her down for medical school! Raw anger still burned when she thought about it.

For an hour she'd dashed about the bungalow, cleaning, sorting, packing. How dared he write to her? But as she'd tried to calm her emotions through work Zanne had remembered something else. There had been an undoubted attraction between them. She'd hated herself for having to admit it. But it was true.

She'd fished out the bits of twisted card, smoothed them and stuck them together with clear tape. Then she had read the message.

Dear Zanne Ripley,

   Had a good conference, got in some excellent climbing and even managed to wear my dinner jacket. If you promise not to shout at me I'll tell you about it when I get back.

   Best wishes, Neil Calder.

Clever so-and-so, Zanne had thought to herself. He can find some other nurse to impress. I'll never meet him again. But the card had remained on her mantelpiece until she left and she'd found herself wondering about him. If only things had been different. . .

Carefully Zanne eased on the elastic knee bandage, then looked up at the anxious face above her. 'How does that feel, Mr Kent? Not too tight? Just enough support to be comfortable?'

'It feels good, Sister.' The man stood and took a few tentative steps round the little surgery. 'This will really help tomorrow. We're going up to—'

Zanne cut in. 'I'm sorry but I think tomorrow you'd better go out with the B group, not the A group.'

The man looked crestfallen. 'That idle bunch! But, Sister, I've been with the A group all week. I'm A group material.'

'If you go out with them tomorrow you'll certainly wreck your knee and probably suffer with it for the next six months. And that would be a pity.' She smiled. 'This is pleasure, not business, you know.'

The grey eyes glanced at her, the mouth hardened and she remembered quickly who this man was. Greg Kent was part-owner and managing director of a firm employing over five hundred men. It was just hard to think of a man in blue shorts and sweater as a captain of industry.

'I know you're right, Sister,' he said after a while. 'I just don't like failing a challenge.'

Zanne flicked through a pile of forms. 'For your age, Mr Kent, you're doing exceptionally well. Far better than most. I don't think you should consider this as failing a challenge.'

Mr Kent was obviously pleased. 'Far better than most? Well, that's good. That's good. Tell me, am

I still all right for the canoeing tests on Friday?'

'Perfectly all right. It certainly won't strain that knee. You can swim, too, as much as you like.'

But he was more interested in canoeing—there was competition involved. 'I expect to do well at canoeing. I've got a boat, you know—it develops strong arms.'

'You'll be all right.' Zanne rose. 'Don't forget. Take it easy tonight. And if your knee starts to hurt again— whatever you're doing, stop it.'

'Don't worry, Sister. I'll do as you say.'

She smiled wryly to herself as he left. Of all the various groups that made up her clients at the hall, middle-aged businessmen gave her greatest trouble. In spite of the talk she gave them at the beginning of the course, and the very careful attention paid by the staff, most of them still tried to do too much. They were vastly competitive. Sprains, strains, bruises—even one nasty case of sunburn—all came from overdoing things.

Zanne stood and stretched, feeling the blood course through her limbs. Official surgery time was over. She would have a late-morning cup of coffee. She loved coffee. It was nice that she didn't have to drink Ward 17 instant any more; she could take the time to grind and percolate her own. The equipment was a farewell present from the ward.

While the aromatic liquid slowly dripped through the filter she turned to the list of the next fortnight's intake to see if any of them required special medical care.

She liked working here; it was casual but efficient. There was time to talk to people—which she loved. And every day was different. Just to prove it, as she reached for her mug there was a loud rapping on the door. Sister was on duty twenty-four hours a day. There was always some little accident or other.

Outside was a broadly smiling Mike Deeley, his arm round a pale-faced girl who held a bloodied hand in front of her. 'Got any sticking-plaster, Sister?' asked Mike.

Zanne saw at once that Mike's flippant attitude was not what the girl needed. She was obviously in pain and was showing early signs of shock. Zanne smiled sympathetically, urged the girl inside and sat her in a semi-reclining chair. Mike followed and leaned comfortably against the surgery wall, obviously intending to stay.

'What happened?' Zanne asked him crisply.

'We were down on the rope garden. When I saw how badly it was bleeding we both ran straight here.'

'You ran?' Zanne tried to keep her voice level. The rope garden was three-quarters of a mile away. 'What made the cut?'

'A sticking-out bit of one of those old metal fences. Not very clean, I'm afraid. Sheena here was in a hurry, tripped and put her hand out to save herself.'

'OK, you can go, Mike. I'll see to this. Sheena won't be available for the rest of the day. And with a cut like this you should have driven Sheena, or at least let her walk slowly. Remind me to tell you all about shock some time, Mike.'

Looking displeased, Mike walked out and Zanne grinned to herself. She seemed to spend half her time shouting at Mike; he tended to be a bit thoughtless. Still, she liked him.

Sheena was about eighteen, dressed in a muddy

tracksuit with her hair tied back. She looked even paler than before and, though she shivered slightly, her face had the sticky sheen of sweat. Shock, Zanne thought.

She fetched two blankets and tucked them round the semi-recumbent body, placing the injured hand carefully on a pad on Sheena's lap. 'Do you like coffee?'

When the girl nodded Zanne fetched her a cup, adding three spoonfuls of sugar and plenty of milk. 'Drink this—it's good for you. Now, don't worry. You can stay with me for a while and I'll dress the cut. It doesn't look too serious and we'll soon have it seen to.' She stayed by the girl, chatting pleasantly.

After a while a slight touch of colour came back to Sheena's cheeks. The warmth, the drink and the comfort were working. Blood was beginning to circulate round her limbs again. When she was sure that her patient was more comfortable Zanne slipped away to check the detailed medical form that all the younger people had to fill in. There were no special problems and quite a recent date for the last tetanus injection. Things should be straightforward.

She took Sheena's pulse. It was still fast and thready, but not as bad as Zanne suspected it had been when the girl came in. Fetching a kidney bowl and warm water with a mild antiseptic, Zanne gently bathed the hand. Under the caked blood and grime there was a nasty, jagged cut across the palm. Noticing Sheena's indrawn breath, Zanne carefully injected lignocaine round the wound and waited for the anaesthetic to take effect. 'That'll cool it and take the pain away,' she said kindly.

Upon closer examination it turned out that the cut wasn't too deep. Zanne managed to pick out a couple of splinters of rust, then was reasonably certain that everything was clean. She thought for a minute and then decided that superglue would be better than stitches or skin closures.

'You're going to stick my hand together?' Sheena asked incredulously.

Zanne winked at her. 'One of the miracles of modern science,' she said. 'Now, just lie there and try to sleep for an hour. I'll be next door, so call if you need anything. I'll fix you a dressing later.'

'But, Sister, we're being assessed on rope-work today.'

'The rest of today,' Zanne said sternly, 'you're taking it easy. I'll do the best I can to get you a cushioned dressing so you can take part tomorrow.'

It had only been an objection for form's sake. Zanne knew that Sheena didn't want to get back to the rope garden. The firm warning made her feel better. Pulling the curtains across the surgery windows, Zanne went back to her own little quarters.

The coffee needed warming a little but it was still good. Zanne sat and sipped, and stared out of her living room window. Ward 17 had looked out on another red-brick ward a few yards away. Here there was a vista of lawns and old trees.

She'd been here three weeks now and she loved it. It was a different kind of nursing, it was both harder and easier. Much of the time she was only a resident first-aider, but there had been one or two occasions where her professional knowledge had been really needed.

There were three main groups, who tended not to mix. The youngsters she saw little of; they were tough and kept very much in line by the staff. The businessmen caused her most trouble. They just couldn't realise that a problem with climbing a mountain was solved in a different way from a problem in business. Zanne sighed. The one good thing was that they all seemed to profit by their fortnight.

Most fun were the people on the recreational courses. Many of them were pensioners. This fortnight's course was 'Lakeland History, Literature and Life'. She saw them most mornings, all with notebooks and rucksacks. John Brownlees had told her that this was the course he really enjoyed teaching.

Outside there was a creak of the wooden floor, a polite cough and a tap at the door. A voice called, 'Do my highly trained nostrils detect the aroma of Colombian Mocha?'

She giggled. 'Come in, Alan. I think it's more likely that you looked at the packet in my kitchen.'

Her door opened. 'Detected,' he said mournfully. 'And I thought I was being super-subtle.'

'You wouldn't perhaps like a cup?' she asked archly.

'If you insist. Perhaps, yes, I would. Black, no sugar—just a small cup please.'

'Exactly like last time. I now leave your own special cup on the tray.'

Dr Alan Mitchell was the local GP, a fit sixty-year-old. Zanne had met him three or four times now and liked and respected him. He was locally born and had worked in the district for the past thirty-five years. If there was anything she couldn't cope with, or wasn't certain of, he was the one to consult first.

So far she'd phoned him twice—once to check a pensioner's asthma prescription and once because she'd

listened to a man's chest and wasn't too happy with
what she heard. On each occasion Alan Mitchell had
come round and sorted out her problem.

'I've got a cut hand in the surgery,' she told him.
'D'you want to have a look while I'm warming your
coffee?'

'I'm sure there'll be no problem. But I'll have
a look.'

He returned just as she poured out his drink. 'I wish
we'd had something like that glue thirty years ago.'
He accepted his cup of coffee and sank back into her
easy chair. 'When I started work that hand would have
been stitched with cat-gut. It would have been painful,
and looked a real mess. But now. . .the stuff I used to
build model planes with.'

'I think it's a bit different,' she said. For a moment
they sat, sipping coffee.

His next question rather surprised her. 'You're off
after twelve today, aren't you? Until three?'

She nodded. 'I'm on call all the time, of course. But
John Brownlees is insistent that staff take time off when
they can. Says it stops them getting stale.'

'Have any plans for this afternoon, then?'

She shrugged. 'Nothing special. I could go into town,
but I don't really need to. Why?'

'I just thought you might like to come for a walk
with me.'

'Hmm. Why is it that I get the feeling that you're
plotting? You've got something in mind for me.'

He looked at her, injured. 'Zanne! Would I do that?'

'Certainly you would. But no matter. I'll happily
come for a walk. Give me ten minutes to get changed.'

First there was Sheena's hand to bandage more

thoroughly. She was told to take the rest of the day off and under no circumstances to take part in any activities.

'Come back early tomorrow and I'll put you a thicker dressing on,' Zanne promised. 'Then you can see how you feel. But nothing until then, OK?'

'I don't really feel like it, Sister.'

'That's to be expected. Just sit there and the doctor and I will run you down to the dormitory.'

Then Zanne changed out of her plain blue uniform into well-worn trousers, shirt and boots. Over her arm she carried her anorak. Following house rules, she phoned reception at the hall and told them where she was going and who she was going with. John Brownlees never let any of his staff out on the mountains without this precaution.

Alan Mitchell drove a battered but serviceable diesel Land Rover. It was the best car for the district—at times he had to drive to strange places in evil weather. They dropped a grateful Sheena off and then bumped onto the main road.

Conversation was difficult because of the noise. She contented herself with watching the scenery as they moved from main road to side road to rough forestry track.

After twenty minutes they pulled up in a clearing. To each side of them were trees—a forestry commission plantation stretched above and below them. It was a desolate spot.

Zanne watched Alan walk to the back of his vehicle, take out a rucksack and drop into it his doctor's bag and a large portable car light. 'Bag in case we need first aid, Doctor?' she asked drily. 'Lantern in case it gets dark?'

He smiled complacently. 'Got you wondering, haven't I? There's work for you too. Will you carry this bag?'

He handed it to her. She peered inside and to her surprise saw that it contained tins of food, sugar, dried milk and tea. He said nothing so she decided not to question him.

They set off, not on the main track but on an almost unnoticeable path that led straight up the wooded hillside. The vegetation was thick and damp and it was muddy underfoot. They climbed an old wall. 'There were once four hill farms in this valley,' Alan said thoughtfully. 'Now all gone. The land covered with these rather soulless pine trees.'

'It's a pity,' Zanne agreed. 'What's that? I can smell smoke!'

It was too damp and too early in the year to be dangerous, but she knew how much the forestry commission disliked fires on their land.

'We're nearly there,' Alan said confusingly, and pushed onwards.

They had seen other evidence of the farms that had once worked this hillside—derelict walls that wandered through the woods with no apparent reason. Now they came to something else. There was a tiny clearing, with a stream running across one corner of it. In the shade of a giant tree was a barn. There were no windows but a trickle of smoke came from a chimney. In place of a door was an old blanket.

'Does somebody live here, Alan?' Zanne asked, appalled.

'We're making a call on Corporal Williams. Call him Corporal. I didn't want to tell you about him before you met him. I wanted you to meet him without preconceptions.'

'If he lives there I've already got them,' she muttered. 'I've seen better built pigsties.'

'Corporal Williams!' Alan shouted from the edge of the clearing. 'It's Dr Mitchell. May we come in?' To Zanne he whispered, 'He values his privacy.'

There was no answer. After calling again, Alan shrugged. He led Zanne across the clearing and pushed aside the blanket. They entered. 'Corporal Williams?' Alan asked again.

It was dark inside but slowly Zanne's eyes grew accustomed to the gloom. It was as bleak inside as out. There was no floor, just hard-packed earth and stones. But there was a rickety chair, an old table covered with newspapers and packages and, in one corner, what seemed to be a pile of blankets on a bed. A fire heaped high with ash smoked on the hearth.

Zanne sniffed. The smell wasn't too bad—woodsmoke and the same piney smell as outside. But there was something musty that had to be human.

'Corporal Williams!' Alan snapped, more loudly.

Zanne jumped as the pile of blankets on the bed stirred and moved. A figure slowly sat upright, clad in an army greatcoat and an incongruous Balaclava helmet. A hand pulled off the Balaclava, revealing straggling grey hair and a beard. 'I was just having a sleep, Doctor.'

Zanne got another shock. The voice was cultured, urbane even. Not the kind of voice one expected in these dismal surroundings.

'Yes, well, Nick Cornish phoned me. He said that when he called in you told him you hadn't been too well.'

The figure on the bed waved a dismissive hand. 'Just a touch of the old trouble, Doctor. Rest is all I need. Lungs won't last forever, you know.'

'They'd last longer if you didn't live in this damp atmosphere,' Alan said sharply. 'Have you taken the pills I left?'

'I have indeed.' The old man appeared to think. 'Well, I think I did.'

'Hmm.' Alan was obviously not convinced. 'Antibiotics are worse than useless if you don't complete the course. I've brought my torch, I want to have a look at you. This is Sister Ripley, by the way. Don't let the trousers fool you—she is a proper nurse.'

The old man bowed his head graciously. 'Good afternoon, Sister Ripley.' The lantern flicked on, revealing the stark little room. Zanne looked round and shivered. This might have been all right for animals a hundred years ago. It was not fit for human habitation.

She could tell that Alan had made the preliminary assessment that all good doctors make, based on voice, attitude and general appearance. Now he slipped a thermometer into the old man's mouth and took his pulse. 'Hmm. Could be worse. But, then, could be considerably better. Right, I want to listen to your chest, Corporal.'

The corporal muttered something about interfering with a man's privacy, but agreed to pull open his greatcoat. There were other layers of clothing inside, but eventually Alan managed to get to his bare chest.

Alan frowned as he listened through his stethoscope.

'I thought so. Sister, I'd like you to listen, please.'

It wasn't usually part of a nurse's job, but Zanne was pleased to be consulted. The heartbeat was quite strong—but underneath she could hear a wheezing.

'Congestion?' asked Alan, and she nodded.

'I'd really like you in hospital, Corporal,' Alan said. 'This condition needs treatment. A couple of days and you could be out again.'

'A couple of days and I could be dead,' the old man said vehemently. 'I read in the newspaper that people die in hospital. Besides, the place smells and you're constantly being interfered with. No privacy.'

Alan sighed. 'Very well. I've brought more pills, and I want you to take them three times a day. Can you remember that?'

'There's nothing wrong with my memory,' the old man said huffily, contradicting what he'd said earlier.

'Good. Now, here's a few groceries; make sure you eat regularly.'

'I always do.' He reached for the bag. 'These will do admirably, Doctor, but I insist on paying you.'

'Of course. You owe me two pounds fifteen pence.'

From the depths of his greatcoat pocket the Corporal extracted a handful of coins and carefully counted them out. 'I think that is correct. Now I give you my thanks, Doctor. Good afternoon.'

It was obvious that they had been dismissed. Alan winked at Zanne, picked up his lantern and walked out.

As they tramped back towards the car Alan said, 'Go on, tell me that he should be in hospital or sheltered accommodation.'

She shook her head. 'No way. He's happy; he's not seriously ill. And he's right. People do die in hospitals.'

'Don't say that out loud—it's a trade secret. Now, why did I bring you?'

She grinned. 'Not very cunning, are you? You want me to keep an eye on him.'

'Just for the next three or four weeks, Zanne. We're a bit short-staffed and it's a long way for me to get to him. Nick Cornish is the local forestry commission man. He drops in on the corporal but he often isn't in this part of the woods. And he's not medically trained.'

'My first responsibility must be to work. But I could call a couple of times a week,' she said.

'Good. If you're in any doubt then phone me. I'll have him in hospital whether he likes it or not.'

'You'd never get an ambulance down there,' she said mischievously.

'Don't tell me. I couldn't even get a helicopter there.'

They reached his car. As they slung their bags in the back he asked, 'How d'you like practising medicine in the country?'

'Well,' she said, 'it's different and I love it.'

Zanne sat at her dressing-table and finished brushing her long hair. Then she carefully applied make-up, a light lipstick and just a hint of mascara. Lastly she carefully wriggled into her dress, a rich cherry-coloured silk. A couple of last-minute adjustments, a pair of black kid-leather pumps and she was ready.

Looking in her full-length mirror, she decided that she didn't look at all bad. Festive, but not over the top. For the past fortnight she had worn nothing but her blue sister's uniform or the usual tracksuit. She'd felt like a change—like dressing up. There was an excuse—she was going to a sort of party—but really she just felt like a change.

It was Friday night—to many of the staff it was Stag's Head night. There were quite a few younger people at the hall and Zanne had fallen into the same easy relationship with them as she had with her climbing friends at home. On Friday night they usually went to the Stag's Head as a group.

Watched by the approving eye of John Brownlees, they all climbed into a minibus. A non-drinking member was driving. Zanne's dress drew more than a few admiring comments.

It started as a very pleasant evening. There was a lot of conversation and dancing at the little disco; they all had one of the hotel's famous pizzas. Zanne drank white wine spritzers—her normal drink at parties. She was enjoying herself.

The others were, too. She noticed that Mike Deeley—as usual—was drinking too much. Eventually he stumbled over to where she was chatting with one of the other instructors and said, 'What are you doing talking? I want to dance with my girl!'

Zanne had had plenty of experience dealing with drunks on Ward 17; perhaps it wasn't surprising—the way they managed to break bones. She decided quickly that the best thing to do here was avoid trouble.

'I'll dance with you, Mike,' she said, 'but I'm not your girl and don't you forget it.' Then she led him to the floor.

Quite obviously, Mike's idea of dancing was to hold her tightly and sway a little. Zanne's idea was quite different. Every time he tried to pull her to him she spun out of his reach, legs and arms moving rhythmically. 'Come on, Mike! Get with it.' After a while Mike got the idea, and tried.

However, she was glad when the record finished spinning. 'Stay on?' Mike asked hopefully.

'No, thanks. I have to go to the loo.' She knew this usually worked.

'Come for a bit of a walk after?' he persisted.

'I've done enough walking this week. I just want to talk to my friends.'

She thought he'd finally got the message. 'Fine, fine,' he said, and walked over to the bar. Zanne went and joined the biggest group she could find.

'Mike being his usual trouble?' asked one of the girls who worked as a chef.

Zanne shook her head. 'Nothing I can't handle. He's a nice lad and I like him. He's just. . .overtired.' The group laughed.

It took a bit of organisation to avoid sitting next to him on the way back, but the other girls cooperated and Mike seemed to be settling down anyway. When they arrived at the hall they all went to the games room—but Zanne cried off. She said she'd have an early night.

But she didn't want an early night. She was happy working in the hall, but occasionally she remembered that this job would not last for ever; that she had to think of her future. I should have been going to medical school! she thought.

Aimlessly she walked through the public rooms of the hall and eventually settled in the staff lounge. It was a handsome room, panelled in mahogany, with deep leather chairs. For once it was deserted. She picked up a magazine and tried to read.

She didn't hear him come in, he must have tip-toed. But when she stood to pick another magazine, there was Mike Deeley in front of her.

'Alone at last!' he said. And before she realised what he had in mind he had wrapped his arms round her and was kissing her.

Shock made her unable to move for a moment. It wasn't a kiss she wanted, but she was irritated rather than alarmed. Then she heard a click. Both she and Mike turned their heads to look at the opening door.

Zanne's mouth dried. In the doorway stood Neil Calder.

He was the last man Zanne had ever expected to see. For an endless moment they stood frozen in a tableau, Mike not releasing her, she open-mouthed and Neil with an ironic smile. She couldn't move. But she saw him with piercing clarity. He was dressed in heavy trousers and a blue naval sweater with the sleeves pushed up. She saw sinewy forearms and a light dusting of dark hair. She saw faint lines of fatigue under his eyes. She saw. . .

'Nurse Ripley,' he said. 'How nice to see you making friends so quickly.' Then he turned and was gone. She heard the clatter of his feet on the tiles in the corridor outside.

Suddenly she could move. She pushed off the befuddled Mike and hissed, 'Just get out of my sight.' Then she was out of the door, running down the corridor and calling after the figure in the distance. 'Dr Calder!'

He heard her, stopped and turned just as she caught up with him.

'Dr Calder!' The words came out in a rush—she

had no time to think; to organise her ideas. 'Dr Calder, I am tired and fed up with women being done down and gossiped about. I want you to know something. I was not kissing that man; he was kissing me—and only because he was too drunk to know what he was doing. I will have something to say to him when he's sober!'

She stopped to catch her breath. He stared at her with the same unnerving expression she remembered from that interview—a cold, emotionless, distant expression. And, then, she thought, there was the faintest sign of his steely face relaxing.

'You know, you don't have to explain yourself to me.'

'I know that. But my reputation is important to me. And a place like this—wrong ideas can get about too quickly.'

Now he was certainly unbending. 'Yes, I know. And I'm sorry for judging you—I'm afraid I did.'

There was another pause and she felt her anger dying. Now she found herself wondering—had she perhaps overreacted? It was nothing much really; she was entitled to kiss who she liked. This man whom she hated, who'd cheated her out of her well-merited place at medical school—who cared what he thought?

And what was he doing here? She'd thought that she'd never see him again and had been quite happy with that.

'What are you doing here?' she asked flatly. 'I thought you were in Chamonix or somewhere.'

'Until this morning I was,' he acknowledged. 'I flew into Manchester this afternoon and drove straight here. Incidentally, is there anywhere I could get a drink? Or a sandwich even?'

She was still a nurse, and now she was closer she could see signs of his fatigue. Even though she disliked the man she felt the urge to help.

'There's a tray left out in the staff lounge,' she said. 'There's tea or coffee and I could make you a toasted sandwich.'

'That sounds like heaven. But don't let me put you out, I could get something myself.'

'Don't tempt me,' she said sharply. 'My Florence Nightingale act sometimes wears a bit thin.'

Fortunately Mike Deeley had gone. As Neil collapsed in an easy chair Zanne moved to the tray and reached for the bread. For the moment she needed to do something; to occupy her brain. She wasn't yet ready to confront the conflicting emotions which seethed inside her.

She made tea and toast, unwrapping the ham, cheese and salad bowl. As she worked she asked her question again, this time a little more calmly.

'You still haven't told me what you are doing here?'

'John Brownlees is an old friend of mine. He'd told me you'd got a place here; in fact, I put up the notice in the hospital that you replied to. Now, that's just what I want.' He accepted a cup of tea.

After sipping appreciatively, he carried on explaining. What he said so shocked her that she thought she'd drop something.

'I'm going to do a bit of my research here. Do some observations, some measurements, on the younger people, before and after their training. They've all volunteered, of course. I want to take blood samples.'

Zanne slowly lowered herself into a chair. 'So you're going to be working here.'

'Working with you, in fact. I'll need your help, especially with the girls on the course.' Did he know what effect this announcement had on her? She wanted nothing to do with this outrageous man. And yet. . .

She handed him his sandwich and poured herself some tea. For a moment she wondered if her cautious two glasses of white wine in the pub had been too much for her. She just couldn't cope.

His cup tinkled in its saucer and he said hopefully, 'I'd love another cup of tea if there is one.' What was she to do?

At that moment John Brownlees bustled into the room, apologising to Neil for being out when he arrived. From the affection shown between them it was obvious that the two were old friends.

'You're in your old room,' John said. 'Wander up when you're ready. Now, I've still got things to do so I'll leave you and see you in the morning. Thanks for looking after him, Zanne.' And he was gone.

Faintly Zanne said, 'I've had a long day. I think I'll go to bed.'

As she rose, Neil also stood up. 'I'm tired, too, after the flight and the drive. But I fancy a breath of air so I'll walk you back to your flat.'

'There's no need,' she said sharply. 'I'll be quite all right.'

'But I want a walk.'

They set off through the trees. It was the last night for various groups and she could hear sounds of merry-making and partying here and there. For some reason, even though she was happy where she was working, Zanne felt suddenly lonely. Her mother was in Canada;

she was miles from the place she'd lived all of her twenty-two years. She shivered.

'You're cold,' he said, and took off the coat he'd picked up. 'Here, put this on.'

'No, honestly, I don't need. . .' But he wrapped it round her anyway.

'Remember the last time I lent you my coat?' he asked mischievously.

In the dark she blushed. 'I remember.'

'How is the young man, by the way? Did he recover?'

'Peter Collins has recovered. Says he'll have another go at walking the rail next year.' Neil laughed.

They reached her front door. Zanne foraged in her bag for the key, then stepped into the shade of her porch. Neil followed her. He reached out, held her gently by the shoulders and turned her towards him.

I hate this man for what he did to me, her brain shrieked, but her body felt something else. He lowered his head and kissed her, softly, sensuously, pulling her to him so that her breasts grazed the front of his sweater. 'Goodnight, Nurse Ripley,' he said. Then he was gone.

Zanne let herself into her little flat. She took off her dress and hung it neatly. She brushed her hair, creamed her face, cleaned her teeth and put out her clothes for the next day. She made herself a mug of tea, though she didn't want it. Then she got into bed and picked up a magazine she didn't want to read.

It was no good. She would have to think about what had happened.

She hated Neil Calder for what he had done to her. But she'd let him kiss her. Worse, she'd responded to him and had been sorry when they'd broken apart. How could she? How could she have such violently opposed feelings towards the man?

She thought she'd never sleep. But the sheer turmoil of her emotions was too much for her. Her eyes closed and her weary brain sought rest.

CHAPTER FIVE

SATURDAYS were always busy at Lawiston Hall. There were groups leaving, groups arriving. Zanne now shared in the general feeling of excitement, saying goodbye to people she'd become friendly with. There was even the occasional feeling of relief at seeing someone go.

She walked over to one of her patients, now looking much more imposing in a dark suit than he had in shorts and sweater.

'Remember, Mr Kent, when you get home you must see a doctor and tell him about your knee. He might want to give you heat treatment or ultrasound, or send you to see a therapist. Don't just forget about it.'

He turned and smiled. 'Truly, Sister, I won't. And thanks for what you've done for me.' He slipped a card into her hand. 'If you ever want a job as an industrial nurse—then give me a phone call. You'd be good at it.'

She shook his hand and moved to the door. John Brownlees came to stand by her and looked at her with approval. 'Another satisfied customer,' he said cheerfully. 'He told me how helpful you'd been, Zanne. Now, can we have a quick word?'

He led her to an old settle. 'Neil Calder,' he said. Zanne looked at him apprehensively.

'I know your duties here are a bit flexible,' John said. 'I told you that you'd be expected to do everything

82

that was necessary, and if that meant an eighteen-hour day you'd have to do it.'

She nodded. 'I'm happy with that.'

'Well, I know you do plenty. But I'm wondering if working with Neil's research group as well is asking too much of you. It certainly wasn't part of the job when you applied for it.'

'Are you saying you don't want me to do it?'

'Not at all. But Neil has asked me to make sure that you had the chance of backing out if you wanted.'

Zanne considered a moment. It was very thoughtful of Neil to give her this chance—and perhaps, for her own peace of mind, she ought to take it. But she knew she wouldn't.

'I'll be happy to work with him,' she said. 'We've met before, you know.'

'So I believe. Look, he's coming up to hear your decision later. Will you give him these two letters?' John smiled and left.

Morosely she looked at the letters she had to hand on. It was a good thing that John hadn't asked her before she saw them. Just ordinary, probably professional letters. But they both were addressed to 'Dr Calder, MB, ChB, FRCS'. She could sign herself S. Ripley, RGN and she was proud of the title Registered General Nurse. But she'd wanted in time to be able to put the words 'Fellow of the Royal College of Physicians' after her name. This man had stopped her.

While she was thinking these disagreeable thoughts the man himself arrived. This time he was dressed in a well-worn grey tracksuit, obviously picked more for use than elegance.

'Zanne, you're going to work with me! Sorry if I

rather took you for granted last night, but I'm really pleased that you'll join us. I think you've got all the right qualities for this job and I think you'll enjoy it. . .'

She smiled to herself as she handed him the letters. She recognised—and rather liked—his obvious enthusiasm and readiness to take advantage of people in what he thought was a good cause. Her mother had the same quality. It was curiously endearing.

He wanted her to come to his initial meeting with the students in an hour's time. She agreed that it would be a good idea, but said she wanted to change into her uniform first. They set off across the grounds together.

It was pleasant knowing that they were going to work with each other. She could handle work and she knew that they could have a reasonable professional relationship. But after a while he said, 'I kissed you last night. Perhaps it was unwise, but I won't apologise because I really enjoyed it and I'd do it again if I could.'

She found his frankness disarming—but there were things he ought to know. She said, 'Believe it or not, in some ways I utterly dislike you. But don't worry, I supposed I didn't really mind being kissed. I managed to put up with it anyhow.'

'You know, you're wonderful for a man's ego,' he muttered, and she had to resist the urge to giggle.

'Be with you in an hour,' she said, and turned off to the surgery.

Outside the surgery was Mike Deeley, obviously waiting and yet trying to pretend that he wasn't. He looked at her uncertainly. 'I had too much to drink last night,' he said, 'and I'm sorry if I upset or embarrassed you. I hope we're still friends.'

He looked so humble that she could hardly stop herself from laughing. But she wasn't going to show it. 'You acted like an ignorant, ill-mannered lout,' she said coldly, and then felt sorry as she watched him wince. 'But I know you didn't mean anything and, yes, we are still friends.' She gave him a friendly kiss on the cheek.

'Thanks, Zanne.' Mike bolted.

Two apologies from presentable young men in one hour, she thought to herself as she buttoned up her uniform. Zanne Ripley, what do you do to men? She giggled again.

In the wooden hut used by the youth group she listened to Neil give his talk. There were about thirty young people there, and assorted leaders. He was a good lecturer, interesting his audience and getting them on his side.

'. . .You know how after you've been exercising hard you often feel good? Well, that's because you've produced a substance called an endorphin. I'm interested in this, and the way it affects you. . .'

He explained that he wanted them to give a blood sample now, and then give another one after they'd been on a gruelling two-night expedition.

'Sister Ripley here will be helping me. If you've got any problems and you can't find me, then ask her.'

Afterwards Neil and Zanne went back to the surgery and the students passed through in batches of five. All of them had had a medical examination already, but Neil asked them to list the exercise they took regularly and listened to their hearts before and after they did a minute's stepping on and off a high bench. All the results were logged in his laptop computer. Meanwhile

Zanne swabbed arms and took the tiny blood samples he required.

He was good with his charges; she guessed that he'd have a good bedside manner. Each person stepping forward was greeted by name—recognised as an individual. The girls were treated subtly differently from the boys.

It took some time to finish all the tests, and at the end of it Zanne realised that she had taken on quite a large extra workload. Still, she didn't mind. When the last student had left, and Neil was studying his initial batch of results, she made them both a drink.

'Only eight girls and twenty-two boys,' she commented as they drank. 'Are you entirely happy with that?'

He shook his head. 'The experiment would be much more significant if we could have an equal number of male and female—but we have to make do with what we are sent.'

'So science has to give way to society?'

'I'm afraid so. There's not a lot I can do to change things. These young people are sent by firms who tend to have more male trainees than female. This may be wrong or there might be a good reason. Would you suggest, for example, that there should be equal numbers of male and female doctors trained?'

Although she felt instantly angry she had to admire him. He knew how she felt but didn't hesitate to pick a fight with her. Calmly she said, 'I believe everyone should be given an equal chance. I certainly don't want positive discrimination.'

'I can agree with that.'

When she muttered, 'You could have fooled me,' he seemed a little taken aback, but said nothing.

That evening Zanne dined in the main building. John wanted all those people who had just arrived to meet as many of the staff as possible. Unlike the young group who ate in their own canteen, the older members were provided with a hotel-style service.

She felt slight trepidation when she found that she was sitting next to Neil. However, he took the opportunity of asking her more about the courses that were running and she found this neutral topic quite safe. She explained about the managers' course, which alternated seminars on management with days out 'tasting' various mountain activities. He appeared more interested in the general course—a repeat of their popular 'Lakeland History, Literature and Life'.

When she had a moment she checked in her bag. There were three people she had to contact who had sent letters from their doctors, and who would need some medical attention.

At the end of the meal John made a welcoming speech and invited members of staff to introduce themselves. By this time Zanne was used to the little ordeal. She stood and said, 'My name is Zanne Ripley and I don't want to see any of you again.' This usually got a laugh and she went on to explain who she was, where the surgery was and what she could offer. As ever, she ended with a plea for people not to overdo things.

'That was a good speech,' Neil complimented her when she sat down. 'Short and to the point.'

'It's practice. I've given it four times already,' she said casually. However, she was pleased with his praise.

'Do you get many people overdoing it?'

Zanne snorted. 'The managers. They get here and they think they're young again. They bring the stress and competition they have at work.'

'Interesting,' he said thoughtfully. 'What about the others?'

'They're lovely and cause me no trouble at all. They're here to learn and enjoy.' She nodded towards the tables where they were sitting. 'Look at them. The only determination on their faces is to have a good time.' After a pause she went on, 'And there are more females than males.'

He grinned. 'I get the feeling you're trying to tell me something, Sister.'

Dinner was now ending and people were moving from the dining-room to the lounge for coffee. Zanne excused herself and went in search of the three people who required her attention. Miss Evers needed injections once a day. The other two were Mr and Mrs Belling, a couple in their mid-sixties.

It was easy to spot Mr Belling as he was in a wheelchair. Because of her mother, Zanne wanted to make sure that Mr Belling had every help he needed; she knew how even the smallest thing could cause difficulties. However, when she saw Mr Belling's direct gaze, and felt his handshake, she decided that her help wouldn't be needed.

Mrs Belling was a different case. She had cancer of the breast. It was terminal. Her doctor had written to say that all possible treatment had been tried. A few days in the country might do her good. She must keep up her medication and not overtire herself.

Zanne introduced herself and asked if there was any-thing she could do.

Both shook their heads. 'Thanks very much, love,' Mrs Belling said, 'but I've just come out of hospital and I think I've had enough of medical folk.' She smiled to show that there was no insult intended. 'All we want is a quiet time together.'

'Well, if you do need anything—even a chat—then I'm available,' Zanne said. 'Reception will always find me. Don't forget—any time, day or night.'

'We'll try not to trouble you,' Mr Belling said.

Zanne left them with their heads together, eagerly studying a book on Lakeland birds. I hope I've got someone to look at me like that when I'm sixty, she thought to herself.

Neil was now sitting on a couch drinking coffee with John. She smiled briefly and was about to pass when John called, 'Got your coffee, Zanne. Sit down; I gather you've had a hard day.'

She looked at Neil expressionlessly, but sat and took her coffee.

'So go on, Neil,' John said, 'tell us what happened to that girl you brought here two years ago. Amy Major, wasn't it? We thought you two were quite close.'

'I'm sorry,' Zanne put in. 'I didn't mean to interrupt a private conversation.' However, she knew that she wanted to stay and listen.

Amiably, Neil said, 'There's no secret. She's now happily married and expecting her first child. You're right, John, we were getting close but I'm afraid she got tired of waiting.'

At that moment one of the staff came over and asked John to come to meet one of the guests. Neil and Zanne were left together. 'Carry on,' she said daringly, 'you've only told half a story.'

He sipped his coffee and went on talking with a humorous sadness that Zanne found fascinating.

'I was in the Mountains of the Moon in Africa for three months. I came home, went to see her and three weeks later was offered a place on an expedition to the Andes. Four months this time. Well, I couldn't turn it down, could I? While I was there she wrote me a "Dear John". Our affair was at an end. She said she felt bad and that soldiers at least had the excuse that they had to go to war, but I went because I'd rather travel than stay with her. End of romance.'

Zanne couldn't help asking, 'How did you feel about it?'

'Well, I was sad. But there was nothing I could do.'

'You could have come home. Tried to persuade her to change her mind.'

He sighed. 'I thought of it—I thought very hard. But I wasn't certain. I was very fond of her, but did I love her sufficiently to spend the rest of my life with her? Possibly not. And by the time I'd finished wondering, it was too late.'

He pointed out of the window. The sun was setting and a distant mountain was edged by its red light. 'What's on the other side of that mountain, Zanne?'

'I don't know,' she said, wondering why he asked.

'Neither do I. But I'll find out soon, I'll take an afternoon off and go to see. I've never been able to settle down. If there's a horizon I've got to cross it. If there's a girl—well, so far I've had to leave her behind.'

'It all seems a bit adolescent to me,' said Zanne, brightly.

He winced. 'Why don't you take up counselling? You have this knack of making people feel happy and contented with their decisions.'

'Part of my charm as a nurse. Have you always been this way?'

'Well, yes. I trained in Manchester because at weekends you can get to Wales, Derbyshire or the Lake District. When I qualified I volunteered to work in Africa for six months and I enjoyed it. At the end of that time I was invited to join an expedition as doctor, and since then I've never looked back. That's why I liked this project. I'll manage to combine research with a fair amount of travelling.'

'So, how long will you stay here?'

He shrugged. 'I'll be moving between here and your old hospital for the next four to six weeks. Don't worry, I'll soon be gone.'

'I don't worry,' she said with some irritation. 'Your plans aren't important to me.' But she wondered if that was true.

The next day was Sunday, and she saw nothing of Neil. In the late morning Miss Evers, aged eighty, came for her injection and stayed for a chat. Half an hour later Mrs Bent came to have her dressing changed, but didn't have time to stop as there was to be a talk on bird life in ten minutes. Part of a typical day.

The evening was typical, too. She sighed as a Land Rover drew up outside and one of the managers had to be helped out. He staggered to her door, leaning heavily on Mike Deeley. She took him inside, sat him on her reclining chair and had a quick word with Mike.

'What happened, Mike?'

He shrugged. 'The usual. Big mouth at the bottom—
''I'm as good as anybody; might be forty-seven but I
can still crack it.'' He got more and more tired but he
wouldn't admit it. Eventually he sat down and just
couldn't move. The rest of the group moved on. I took
his pulse and it was too high. So I waited twenty
minutes and then we came down—very slowly.'

'Any pains in the chest?'

'None. No danger of a heart attack. Pains in the side,
of course, but they soon went. When I got him to the
Land Rover I gave him tea with sugar. I'd say just
exhaustion.'

'Sounds like you're right; you've done a good job.'

All the leaders had first aid certificates, and Zanne
had given them a short refresher course. She was
reasonably certain that Mike's diagnosis was correct,
but she had to make sure.

'How d'you feel now?' she asked as she took the
man's pulse.

'Not too good, but a lot better than I did. Is it
my heart?'

She shook her head. 'We'll check, of course, but I
suspect it's nothing so serious. You just overdid it.
Breathlessness. Pains in your side and growing weak-
ness in your legs. Your body couldn't produce
sufficient glycogen to keep you going, so in time it
gave up. You're not used to walking up hills, are you?'

'I'm fit enough,' he mumbled.

'Not quite, I'm afraid. Now, I want you to have
another drink and then stay here and rest for a couple

of hours. Your pulse is fine, by the way.' She fetched him a pile of magazines.

'But I don't feel too bad now; can't I join the others?'

'I really have to be certain about you. Just rest. I'll check you every twenty minutes.' She fetched the sweet tea and then left him.

At nine that night she drove him back to the hall, told him to go to bed and stay there all next day. 'I'll be in to see you at about nine in the morning. Then we can take it from there.'

By this time he was much recovered. 'I've made a bit of a fool of myself, haven't I, Sister?' he asked.

'Certainly not; don't worry about it. Think of it as a valuable experience. You're not the first and you won't be the last to overdo things a bit.' With this encouraging thought, she left him. It had been a typical day.

By the next morning he was much recovered, but still agreed to take her advice and stay in bed for the day. She left, feeling that she'd done a competent job. There were a couple of slight problems in surgery, but they were easily dealt with.

When the last person had gone she walked round her little kingdom, tidying, straightening, preparing. She wondered why this sudden outburst of activity, and made herself face the truth. In an hour she'd be working with Neil again, and she was rather looking forward to it. She tried to pretend that she was only interested in the work they were doing, but she couldn't. She wanted to see him. Since she hated him so much it was a paradoxical state of affairs.

At lunchtime she packed a small bag and walked

down to the climbers' hall. They'd all been on a tough two-night hike, carrying all equipment and scaling three high peaks. On past form there would be the odd blister, sprain or strain, but nothing serious. They were to have a shower and then give a blood sample before eating and taking the rest of the day off.

'Morning, Zanne; nice to see you again.'

It was Neil, in his scruffy tracksuit again, but looking incredibly—well, just incredible. She felt a sudden burst of shyness. 'Morning, Neil,' she mumbled.

'What's in the bag?'

This was professional; she could deal with this. 'Immediate first aid. Plasters and cream for blisters, bandages for joints and antiseptic for cuts and grazes. That should be enough to deal with ninety-nine per cent of medical problems today.'

He shook his head. 'Your efficiency alarms me. All ready for taking blood?'

'It's all set up.' They had decided to take blood in the surgery again.

'They should be coming in about now; let's go to meet them.' Together they moved outside.

After five minutes they saw the trainees walking through the woods towards them. Zanne's experienced eye noted the ones who were limping and the ones who were holding an arm or an elbow. She had a word with each, offering whatever was necessary—to be used after the shower.

As was typical after such a hard couple of days they were all elated, shouting at each other in an almost drunken manner. She and Neil smiled at each other. This euphoria was brought on by endorphins. They both recognised it because they'd both experienced it.

Then Zanne saw something strange. One of the girls looked round, then quietly dived into the bushes. Five minutes later she emerged, pale-faced, and looked round again.

In the general cheerful noise her quietness wasn't noticed. Zanne made her way to the girl and quietly said, 'I want a word with you in surgery now.'

'I'm all right, Sister, truly I am. I just need a shower.'

'Good. But we'll have a little girls' chat. Don't tell anybody; just walk up there.'

For a moment Zanne thought that the girl was going to refuse. But she took one look at Zanne's determined face and decided not to.

The girl's name was Sally O'Neill. She was tall, fair and still pale-faced. In the surgery she moved straight into the attack. 'Really, Sister, it's good of you to bother with me, but there's no need and. . .'

'How long since your last period?' Zanne asked.

There was silence, and then tears. 'I'm about twelve weeks gone,' she confessed eventually, blowing into the tissue that Zanne had offered her. 'But I must do well on this course. I'm the only girl apprentice in our firm; I can't make a fool of myself. Please, Sister, don't tell Dr Calder; I know he'll have me thrown off. And I read in this book that it's all right to do exercises at this stage.'

'Have you told anybody?' Zanne asked.

'Not yet. I was going to when this fortnight was over.'

'You *must* tell somebody,' Zanne insisted. She glanced at the girl's left hand. 'Your parents at least.'

Sally had caught Zanne's glance. 'I am married, you know,' she said. 'I just left my ring off. I wanted to. . .

Sister, please don't tell Dr Calder.'

Zanne sighed. 'Well, I won't right now. Go through there and have a shower and then get into bed in the sick bay. I'll come and see you later.' Sally did as she was told.

Five minutes later Neil turned up with the first batch of the freshly showered trainees. This time there was no time-consuming examination and taking the blood took little more than a minute. Zanne looked at assorted minor injuries, but most of the trainees had managed to deal with them themselves. Meanwhile, Neil took the phials of blood and placed them neatly in order.

There was a lot of noise in the surgery. The trainees were still high on endorphins, and there was much good-natured mockery and abuse. Neil winked at her. 'If we could bottle this stuff,' he whispered, 'we'd make a fortune and ruin the trade in alcohol.'

'If only people knew it was free,' she whispered back. 'All you need is forty-eight hours' pain.'

'Hmm. *Doctors* are supposed to be cynics, not *nurses*.'

Then all the blood had been taken—but for one. 'Where's Sally O'Neill?' Neil asked, looking up from his list. 'Has she come over yet?'

Zanne braced herself. 'I'm afraid Sally won't be giving blood,' she said. 'She overtired herself so I've sent her to bed.'

'I am a doctor, you know,' he said mildly. 'I think I could be relied upon to act responsibly.'

'I'm sorry. It is my professional opinion that it would be best for her welfare if she didn't give blood at present.'

'Your professional opinion?' Now there was anger in his voice.

'That's what I said. Sally O'Neill is in the medical care of Dr Mitchell and myself. You are not her doctor.'

His face was as still and as cold as stone. 'I still think I could be trusted to form my own medical opinion.'

'There's no need. I have already formed mine. Rest assured, this is a matter I know something about.'

She had met this before. The truly frightening men were those whose voices grew quieter as they grew more angry. Softly Neil said, 'My experiments are important. I will not have them compromised by some stupid girl who is using her menstrual cycle to gain sympathy.'

That did it. Flatly she said, 'As far as I'm concerned, you will not take blood from Sally O'Neill. The girl is in my care. If you try to go against my wishes I shall resign from this post, effective immediately. Now, is there anything else before you leave, Doctor?'

He stood. 'That is the typical threat of an unsure, emotionally unstable woman. I will certainly not try to go against your wishes. God knows what you might do if I did. Good afternoon, Sister!'

Zanne went and banged open her kitchen door. She was shaking with anger—but she was also upset. For once in her life she felt like taking one of the tranquillisers that some of her patients swallowed like sweets. She'd just realised how much Neil's good opinion mattered to her. It angered her that it should.

After a while she went to check up on her patient. Sally O'Neill was asleep. Zanne looked down on the silent form and wondered if she realised what trouble she was causing. It was bad enough dealing with illness

and injury, without having to cope with emotional stress
as well.

Then she phoned Alan and told him what had happened. 'Difficult,' came the thoughtful voice down the
phone. 'But I think you are right. The girl is certainly
entitled not to give blood, and she's also entitled not
to have to explain why. Just one thing, Zanne. Try to
persuade her to phone her husband. D'you want me to
come to see her?'

'There's no need, Alan. I'll get in touch if there is.'

An hour later, when she looked in on Sally again, the
girl was looking much better. There was colour in her
cheeks and more determination in her voice. Zanne
fetched her some soup.

'Now, Sally,' she said when the soup was finished,
'we've got to work out a plan. First of all I think you
ought to phone your husband. Then you can sleep here
tonight and we can plan what's going to happen to
you then.'

'But I wanted to do this course first! Then I was
going to tell him.'

'You love him, don't you?' Zanne asked gently.
'And he loves you? Don't you think he ought to be
involved in any decisions you make?'

Tears ran down Sally's face. 'I suppose so. It's just
that—I was so proud of being the apprentice selected
to come on this course. And now I've failed because
I'm a woman.'

'You've not failed,' Zanne told her. 'And, remember,
you're going to do something that no man has ever
done. Now, you can ring the switchboard from this

phone and they'll connect you with home. I'll be in to see you in another hour.'

Feeling unaccountably depressed, Zanne put on her coat and walked out of the surgery. First she had to go to the main building to pick up mail and check that a delivery had been made. Then she decided that she didn't want to go straight back to the surgery.

She was fed up with people and their problems, she thought. She wanted to get away. Then she realised that it was her own problems that were worrying her. That was annoying. Carefully picking up her route to avoid meeting anyone, she crossed the hall's grounds and headed for the seldom visited top corner. The sun would set soon. She'd sit and watch it in peace.

There was a log where she occasionally sat, facing the sweep down into the valley below and up to the mountains beyond. There was one dark peak high above the others. Neil Calder had said that he wanted to see what was on the other side of it. The sooner he goes looking the better for all of us, she thought.

But slowly her anguished spirit calmed. There were bird calls, and the faint rustling of the wind in the branches around her. She could smell the resin in the nearby pine trees and feel the breeze on her warm face. She responded to the solitude and peace.

It was the bird which gave him away. One moment there was the usual song, then the piercing screech of an alarm call. Someone was coming. Behind her Zanne heard the brushing of feet in long grass. She didn't turn. But somehow she knew who it was.

An amused voice said, 'You can't ignore me; you know I'm here. I saw your body stiffen.'

She felt it stiffen even more. Coolly, without turning,

she said, 'Very perceptive, Dr Calder. Now I am off duty. So, unless it's important...'

'Get lost, Dr Calder. Perhaps I ought to. In fact, I saw you walking this way and I followed you. And this is important, if only to me.'

He came to sit on the end of the log, well away from her. She still didn't look at him.

After a while he said, 'Sally O'Neill has just been to see me. She told me that she's pregnant and that she'd insisted you didn't tell me. I've had a word with her husband, who seems a very nice chap; he's coming up tomorrow and we're all going to have a chat.'

'Sounds very cosy,' Zanne said, feeling a fresh flow of anger.

'I've said that we can make arrangements for her to finish the course or, if she wants to go home, I'll try to arrange for her to come back next year.'

'That's very good of you.'

'No, it's not,' he said sharply. 'You should have known that would be the attitude I would have taken.'

Reluctantly, she said, 'I suppose so.'

'But what's really bad is that you detected something that I didn't. Worse than that, I didn't have faith in you and your medical abilities. You certainly couldn't break a medical confidence, and you acted properly— professionally. And I was a loud-mouthed boor.'

'True,' she said with some satisfaction.

He sighed. 'Well, you were right and I was wrong and I apologise.'

There was a silence that she was unable to break.

Then he stood and said, 'Well, I'll leave you to your thoughts. Goodnight, Zanne.'

'You don't have to go,' she said jerkily. 'You can

sit her for a while. And your apology's accepted, of course. Just forget about it.'

'That I can't do. And I have to go—there are some results I have to collate.' He hesitated. 'Just one more thing. Will you have dinner with me tomorrow evening? Just so I can be certain you've forgiven me?'

'I'll be free at eight,' she said.

'Ideal. I'll pick you up at eight-fifteen. Goodnight.' Then he was gone.

The sun was now low, a great orange ball behind the jagged outline of the hills. She stared, hoping that the beauty of the scene would dispel her whirling thoughts.

This man had wounded her grievously. She *knew* she was entitled to a place in medical school. He'd rejected her without good cause. Now she found herself working with him, even going to dinner with him. She was discovering that under that spiky exterior there was a man who could be witty, charming, thoughtful. She really liked him, even. . .

Her life had been easier when he'd been just an object of her hate.

CHAPTER SIX

NEXT morning John Brownlees rang just after ten. He sounded concerned. 'Zanne, d'you remember Mr and Mrs Belling? He's the man in the wheelchair.'

'Of course I do. A lovely couple.'

'Yes, well. . .' She could tell that John was uncertain about something. It wasn't like him.

'You know it's our policy not to interfere. People come here for a holiday and they're entitled to be left alone. It's just that so far Tom and Grace have been up first thing every morning. They're everyone's friends; they're loving the course. But this morning Tom came and asked if he could take a breakfast tray in for Grace. He said they wouldn't be going on the coach trip, even though we know they were looking forward to it last night. I just wondered. . .'

'I'll come straight up and call in on them. I'll think of some excuse.'

'Thanks, Zanne. Appreciate it.'

Before walking up to the main house, Zanne unlocked her filing cabinet and reread the letter from Grace Belling's doctor. Then she turned to one of her thick medical textbooks. It wasn't a nurses' textbook—it was for doctors. She had bought it in the hope—in the anticipation—of being a medical student.

As she picked it up, yet again she felt the familiar flash of anger. She deserved a place in medical school! She had half conquered her initial deep distress, but there was still a great resentment.

Grace Belling's problems were much greater. She had cancer of the breast. There was a short case history in the textbook, and Zanne read how a mastectomy had not proved sufficient. Now, for a while, Grace was symptom-free, but it was obvious that she couldn't last much longer. Her medication was simply to ease pain. Sighing, Zanne packed a small bag and walked up to the hall.

Tom Belling's expression was strained when he opened the door to Zanne's tap, but he still managed a smile. 'It's Sister Ripley, isn't it?'

Zanne had decided to be blunt. 'We're worried about Grace,' she said. 'Is she ill?'

Unsuccessfully Tom tried to maintain his smile. 'She's just tired,' he said. 'We thought a day in bed might be a good idea. We didn't want to trouble anyone.'

'It's no trouble to me. Shall I have a look?'

When she stepped forward Tom had to give way. Zanne thought she saw an expression of relief on his face.

The breakfast tray was by the bed, largely untouched. Grace was half-upright in bed, supported by pillows. Tom had pulled back the curtains, and she was gazing desperately at the sun shining on the trees outside. When Zanne saw her face she knew that something was wrong.

'Hello, my dear,' Grace said. 'It's good of you to call.'

Zanne took Grace's temperature and pulse and asked her how she felt.

'Well, just a little bit of pain. And this morning I

felt so incredibly tired. I just didn't have the strength to get out of bed.'

'You're taking all your medication?'

'Of course I am! Tom sees that I do.'

'I think you've had a slight relapse,' Zanne said carefully. 'I'll phone the doctor; he might want you to go into hospital.'

'No.' The voice was remarkably firm. 'I know I'm dying, Sister. And I'd rather have six weeks of this than fritter away three months in a hospital bed. Tom agrees, don't you?'

'Yes.' It was only one word but Zanne's heart went out to the feelings hidden in it.

'Well, we can't just leave you here like this. I'll go and phone Dr Mitchell. He might have some advice.'

Zanne hurried to Reception, more affected than she liked to admit. She had nursed patients before who died. Sometimes it was harder to take than others.

'What dosage is she on at the moment, Zanne?'

Alan's voice was crisp and professional. It was just what Zanne needed.

'She's on morphine.' Zanne read out the dosage from the phial in her hand.

'Hmm. She ought to be at hospital, or at least at home.'

'I know that. But she's so enjoying it here.'

'Right. Double the dose of morphine. It'll give her a boost. It's swings and roundabouts, Zanne. We're cutting down on her time alive, but making sure she enjoys what time she has left. And I'll drop in this afternoon.'

'Thanks Alan. I'll go and tell them at once.'

The increased dose worked wonders. Zanne went to

work in the library for an hour and then returned to find Grace up and dressed, eyes sparkling.

'I feel much much better. Tom and I thought we'd go for a walk round the grounds.'

'I'll come with you,' said Zanne, wondering if Grace might relapse again as quickly as she'd recovered.

'Good. We want to go down and watch the young people. We haven't been there yet.'

As Zanne and Grace walked slowly along the path to the trainees' camp, Tom rolled his wheelchair ahead. The surface here was metalled and he could make good speed.

'He's very strong in the arms and chest,' Grace said proudly. 'He enjoys getting out. He's done two marathons, you know.'

'My mother's in a wheelchair,' Zanne said. 'It's hard at first, but if you don't let it beat you there is a lot you can still do. Mind you, that's easy for us to say.'

'Yes. I can remember Tom's frustration after the accident. But he manages.'

They stopped and sat on a bench, where Tom was waiting for them. Ahead of them was the small rock outcrop that the trainees used for climbing practice. At the moment they were abseiling, sliding down the rock face on ropes under the watchful eyes of Mike Deeley and Neil.

'I always fancied doing that,' said Tom wistfully, 'but I never got round to it. And, then. . .' He indicated his wheelchair.

'There are other things you can do,' Zanne said. 'Grace has just been telling me about your marathons.'

'I enjoy them.' He grinned. 'And I wear the medal I get round the house for a week afterwards.'

Neil had noticed them, and was loping over towards them. Zanne felt her heart beat just a little faster as he approached. Whether it was irritation with him or some other emotion, she didn't really know.

There were introductions and small talk. Then Zanne said flatly, 'All his life Tom here has wanted to abseil. But he can't; he's in a wheelchair.'

Neil looked at her, and she knew that he could read her thoughts. 'Don't go yet,' he said, 'but I must just go and have a quick word with Mike.'

After that it seemed simple—though Zanne knew that it wasn't. Neil came back with Mike and four of the trainees. Grace and Zanne sat on the bench while Tom went with them, wheeling his chair to the bottom of the climb. There was a path up behind the outcrop, but Zanne noticed that Neil only helped Tom when it was necessary.

Eventually the wheelchair was perched backwards on the very edge of the cliff. Nervously, Grace clutched Zanne's arm. But they could both see the red safety ropes holding both Tom and the chair.

The chair was eased over the lip of the rock. Neil was to one side, acting as safety man. And slowly the chair descended the sheer face.

'Look,' Zanne said. 'The trainees are taking the weight of the chair. But Tom's taking his own weight. He's abseiling himself.'

The wheelchair reached the bottom of the cliff, and the trainees took it and set it upright. There was a little knot of people talking there for a few minutes, and then Tom and Neil came back up the path.

'You've made him so happy,' Grace said. Zanne passed her a tissue to wipe away a stray tear.

Neil and Tom arrived, and for a moment there was silence. 'I'm glad I've seen you do that, Tom,' Grace said eventually.

'I'm glad I've done it.' Tom stuck out his hand. 'Thanks, Neil. I hope you know what it meant to me.'

'I can guess,' Neil said briefly. 'Now, I must get back. Come and see us again.'

It was a more contented group of three that moved back towards the hall.

'He's a nice young man,' Grace said suddenly to Zanne. 'Is he a special friend of yours?'

She shook her head. 'Not really. Just someone I work with.'

Grace smiled. 'He's more than that. You didn't see him looking at you. I did.'

She wouldn't add to this remark.

What should she wear? Dinner with a man she had cause to dislike but couldn't help liking. It was a problem. She half wished she could go in uniform. Her uniform made a statement about her—she was Sister Ripley, a qualified nurse, cool, competent at her job.

Without being vain, she also knew that the plain blue emphasised her figure and drew attention to the graceful way she moved. She remembered a couturier on TV once saying that for a beautiful woman the most flattering garment was the simplest.

She didn't want to overdress, or wear something too clingingly feminine. It might give the wrong signals. In the end she grew quite bad-tempered with herself when she realised how much time she'd spent thinking about how to dress to please him. He wasn't worth it!

And she hadn't brought too much from home anyway. She ran herself a bath.

She was ready when he walked up the path. He was wearing a light grey suit with a darker blue shirt and tie. He looked well, neither formal or informal.

When she opened the door to him she realised that she'd made a good decision about her own dress. She could tell by his eyes that the compliment he paid her was sincere. 'Zanne, you look gorgeous,' he said.

She was wearing black velvet trousers and a white silk sleeveless top. She knew that her arms were one of her best features—shapely and yet not too muscled. Round her left wrist she wore her favourite bangle— parallel strips of silver and white enamel.

His car was a Jaguar. She revelled in the smoothness of the ride, the rich smell of leather and even the background sound of Vivaldi on the stereo.

'You're quiet,' he said.

'I was just thinking—I love the life up here, bouncing over moors in the Land Rover, wearing my boots and anorak. But every now and then a bit of luxury is very pleasant.'

'This is luxury?'

'If not, it'll do for me.'

It was dusk now; the last rays of sun flashed through the trees and then fast-moving shadows gathered round them. The mountains cut off the last of the sun. She felt warm and protected in the car.

'Where are we going?' she asked.

'We're going to the Red Lion, at Taggart. It's just a pub, you know. Quite simple.'

'I'm sure it is,' she said. But something about his

smile made her doubt that he was telling her the full truth.

They drove for perhaps twelve miles, the last four on twisting back roads. Then they climbed a steep hill, and just below the summit was the Red Lion. She suspected from the cars in the car park that this was not just a simple pub. Perhaps it had been once. The grey stone building was certainly old, but it had been renovated with considerable taste.

Once they stepped inside the front door her suspicions were vindicated. The foyer was tasteful and elegant in oak panelling and red carpet.

'Neil! Good to see you, old friend!' A large man stepped towards them, thrust a bundle of leather-bound menus onto a convenient table and embraced Neil.

'It's good to see you too, Oscar. May I present my good friend Sister Ripley—but Zanne to her friends.'

Oscar took her hand. 'Zanne?' he questioned.

She had to smile. Oscar's ebullient personality would charm anyone. 'My real name is Suzanne,' she explained. 'I'm not sure why everyone shortens it.'

'Suzanne is a beautiful name, and it suits a beautiful lady. You will be Suzanne to me. Now, before you dine I have a split of champagne waiting at the bar. We will have just a glass.'

Oscar led them to a table in the bar. The minute they were seated a waiter appeared and poured three glasses of sparkling wine. Zanne had never had such service before. Oscar sat and drank with them for five minutes, but she noticed that his eyes were constantly flicking round. He needed to check on everything.

After five minutes he rose and said, 'I must run my restaurant. *Bon appétit*, I will see you later.' And he was gone, moving smoothly and swiftly among his guests.

'What a nice man. Is it his restaurant?' Zanne asked.

'It's his. He's built it up to this practically single-handed. There isn't a job here he can't do, from commis-chef to wine-buyer.'

'How did you get to meet him?'

'Ah. If I tell you, I'm acting unethically. Disclosing the name of a patient. In fact, I was climbing in the Langdales when Oscar's son had rather a bad fall and broke his leg. Fortunately I got there just as his pals were about to carry him down the mountain. We had quite a heated argument, which was difficult as it was snowing at the time. They wanted to cart him straight off; I wanted to do a bit of emergency setting before they did.'

'Who won the argument?' Zanne asked, fascinated.

'I think I did. Anyway, I set young Arthur's leg as best I could. Later on I met Oscar by his bedside. Arthur introduced us, Oscar invited me for a meal and we've been friends ever since.'

'Your table is ready, Dr Calder.' From somewhere a *maître d'hôtel* had appeared.

'It's beautiful,' Zanne gasped as they were led into the dining-room. Once it had been a barn. Now one entire wall had been removed and replaced by glass. They seemed to hang over the vast, dark panorama of the valley below, with even a distant glimpse of the sea. Their table for two was by the window—she thought it the best table in the house.

'The menu, sir.' And they were left alone.

'I'm hungry,' she said. 'What shall we have?'

Neil pursed his lips. 'I always like to try to eat what's local,' he said. 'I can't stand people who want chips

in the Himalayas, or hamburgers in the Andes. I've
always tried to choose something native.'

'And have you always been happy with your
choice?'

He looked mournful. 'To be frank, no. In fact, in the
Himalayas I had something which I believe was yak
stew. It was horrible!'

She laughed. 'So what have you had that you particularly enjoyed?'

'In South America I had a delicious thick soup with
herbs and pieces of chicken meat.' He paused for effect.
'Only the chicken turned out to be snake.'

'We'll see what Oscar has to offer,' she said firmly.
'I don't think he'll have snake soup.'

They both started with potted shrimps, culled from
the bay that morning. The brown bread was home-
baked and the butter from a local farm. Zanne asked
Neil to choose the wine and, to her surprise, he ordered
a half-bottle of Sancerre just for her. 'I'm going to
have beer,' he explained.

'Beer?'

'It's a local brew and it's excellent. Besides, I've
got to drive home. I don't want too much alcohol
inside me.'

She ordered local grilled trout for her main course,
and once again was surprised at his choice. 'You're
eating sausages? Not duck or ham or beef?'

He exchanged glances with the *maître d'hôtel*. 'Oh,
yes, Zanne, I'm eating sausages. But what sausages!
These didn't come from the supermarket. Locally made
again, you know.'

She still thought it a strange choice. But just before
their main course was served the waiter put a plate in

front of her with four small rings of what appeared to be grilled sausages. 'A taster, ma'am. With the chef's compliments.'

She looked at Neil, picked up the fork and tasted. Then she tasted again. 'Oh, I see,' she said. Gloomily she realised that the common British breakfast sausage would never taste the same again.

It was a pleasant meal and he was an interesting companion. On some topics he was self-assured, certain. On others he was happy to be persuaded that he was wrong. She thought she'd never spent so long with a man with such a quirky mind.

They finished with fruit and coffee. She found herself warming to him; he was a good conversationalist and the meal had been truly memorable. 'Thank you for a lovely meal and evening,' she said after they'd said goodnight to Oscar. 'I can't remember when I've enjoyed myself more.'

'The evening's not over yet,' he said as he handed her into the car.

She felt a faint shiver, half fear, half anticipation. 'What d'you mean?' she asked, more sharply than she had intended.

He remained calm. 'It's still quite early and there's a beautiful moon.'

She felt slightly let down. 'So, where are we going?'

'Let me surprise you.' He wouldn't say any more.

After fifteen minutes' driving she saw the silver reflection of the lake on her right. Then they turned towards it. 'Are we going to the yacht club?' she asked. She'd been once before, and had enjoyed it.

'Not exactly,' he said, but he parked in their car park. Then he led her towards the little marina and unlocked the gate. Their feet rattled on the wooden planks as he took her to the end of one of the jetties. He stooped and cast off the rope attached to the bows of what seemed like a largish cruiser. 'Welcome aboard the *Lady Helen*,' he said, and handed her down into the cockpit. A minute later they were chugging softly onto the silver waters of the lake.

'A boat ride!' she breathed. 'It's magic at this time of night.'

'It's also getting cold.' He dived into the cabin. 'Here, put this on.' She was handed a thick coat.

For a while she was content just to enjoy the beauty of the lake and mountains, but then curiosity got the better of her. 'Is it your boat?' she asked.

'Partly—other people can use it as well. It actually belongs to my parents, they've had it for years. I spent a lot of my youth on this boat.'

She wondered what he'd been like as a boy. It was impossible to imagine a ten-year-old Neil in short trousers. 'Are your parents still alive?' she asked tentatively. 'Do they live round here?'

He laughed. 'My father was a local GP, and my mother a midwife. I think in their case inheritance worked backwards. They caught wanderlust from me. They've just spent a year with my younger brother who's a vet in New Zealand, and they've decided to settle there. Four grandchildren, you know.'

'So you disappointed them? No grandchildren at home?'

'Afraid so. But they haven't given up hoping. They say they'll come back when the first one is due. I don't know whether that's a threat or a promise.'

She wondered what Neil's children would be like. . .

It was pleasantly intimate, sitting together with him in the dark cockpit, seeing only the silver of his profile in the moonlight. He took her hand, held it under his and made her move the tiller so that she could feel the responsiveness of the boat. 'A boat is alive,' he told her. Didn't he know that she was more conscious of the life in his hand?

They moved slowly into the centre of the lake. Around them was the silver of the water and the moon-bleached mountains, speckled with the tiny lights of farms.

She shivered, and it seemed natural that he should put his arm round her. Then it seemed equally natural that he should bend his head and kiss her.

At first his kiss was light, almost hesitant. But when she slipped her arm round his shoulders and pressed herself to him she could feel the urgency throb through his body. For what seemed like an infinity she lay there cradled in his arms, alive to nothing but the magic of his kiss. His mouth roamed her face—his lips sometimes teasing, sometimes cajoling, sometimes urgently demanding.

She didn't know how, but his hand had stolen inside her jacket and was stroking the inside of her arm. His touch was so gentle that she waited half-impatiently for him to open the buttons on her blouse and caress the slopes of her breasts.

Time passed, unmeasurable. She was content with what she had, with where she was. Then there was the sudden cold touch of something on the back of her neck. Her eyes flicked open. The moon had disappeared. She heard a noise like paper ripping in the distance—the sound of rain on water. Another drop landed on her arm.

'This is the Lake District,' he said ruefully. 'It always rains when you don't want it to. Perhaps it's only a squall.'

Nearby was an island, a little clump of trees apparently growing out of the water. Neil directed the boat towards it, and after a moment there was the gentle scraping sound of the boat grounding. Neil cut the engine. 'We'll be all right here till the rain passes,' he said. 'Let's go inside the cabin.'

It was an old boat, made of wood rather than plastic. Neil lit an oil lamp and she looked with approval as the soft light illuminated brass-bound mahogany fittings. He sat beside her on a couch covered with soft red cloth. And, as the rain suddenly banged and rattled on the deck outside, he kissed her again.

It was warm in the cabin; both discarded their coats. She looked down at her blouse, open all the way down. 'I feel a fool like this,' she said, and on an impulse shrugged out of it.

He reached for the fastener on her bra. She smiled at the sudden intake of his breath as he eased the lacy garment over her shoulders. 'You're beautiful,' he groaned.

It seemed as if her course was predestined—as if she had no control over the way events were moving. She only knew that this was what she wanted; that this man was for her. She discovered in herself a wantonness she'd never suspected as she opened his shirt to feel the roughness of his chest. He bent to kiss her breasts and her head arched with the excitement of it.

He lowered her backwards, sliding so that they were lying side by side on the couch. Her eyes passed over things of no consequence—a barometer, a picture of a mountain screwed to the bulkhead, a small bookshelf with old books fastened down. She could see the titles—an ancient *Gray's Anatomy*, a *British National Formulary*, textbooks on medicine.

Neil's father must have done some studying on this boat. Or perhaps Neil had himself—the titles were quite recent. Neil was a doctor; his father was a doctor. She was *not* going to train to be a doctor. This man had turned her down!

She said nothing; did nothing. But the very rigidity of her body passed him an unmistakable message. Reluctantly his caresses stopped. A distant part of her mind acknowledged his sensitivity; some men would not have stopped.

'I didn't mean to rush you, Zanne,' he said gently. 'I'm sorry.'

She decided to be honest with him. 'It wasn't that. I just remembered. You're the man who stopped me being a doctor.'

'Ah. I see.' He said nothing more and only his ragged breathing told her what he was going through. She felt the faintest twinge of guilt. She didn't want to be a tease.

She felt worse when he turned his back so that she could pull on her bra and blouse. He's a gentleman, part of her brain said. But he stopped you being a doctor! retorted another. She felt bewildered.

The rain thudded on the cabin roof, undiminished. They sat side by side in uncomfortable silence. Then he began to tell her about one of his climbing trips; she was glad that he at least could say something.

He told her about one of his first expeditions in the Himalayas when he'd been camp doctor. They'd been at camp seven, the one immediately below the summit.

'Two men were going to make the final push for the summit next day. One was Jonathan Gash, very experienced but now getting just a bit old for that kind of thing. This was to be his last major expedition and he wanted to finish in a blaze of glory.

'Anyway, I saw him limping. I got him to my tent and looked at his feet. Both had frostbite—there was definite vesiculation and, I thought, oedema. I warmed his feet and he told me there was nothing wrong— he'd just had his boots too tight. The sensation had only just come on. I thought he'd been suffering for some time and had kept quiet, but he swore this wasn't true. You see the point. If vasoconstriction had only just occurred then he was fit to climb, but if it had occurred some time ago—then he was in danger and should not climb.'

Zanne wouldn't have thought it possible after what had just happened, but she was now quite interested in the story. 'Go on,' she said. 'What did you do?'

'Remember, this was my first high-altitude expedition, and I was only a callow doctor. But I went to the expedition leader and told him that if Jonathan made the climb next day he'd probably lose both feet. Jonathan said this was rubbish and that the discomfort had just started. The expedition leader had to choose between my expertise and the possibility that an old friend was lying. He chose to believe me and sent someone else on the final assault. Jonathan Gash never forgave either of us.'

'And were you right?'

'Yes,' he said flatly. 'But Jonathan never thanked me for saving his feet.'

It suddenly struck her that Neil had had a specific reason for telling her this story. Angrily she said, 'You're hinting that it's not your fault I got turned down for medical school. That's unfair because I know what happened in that interview, never mind medical confidentiality. It's irrelevant now, but one of the three members on that committee was my boyfriend. He told me you rejected me.'

She could tell that he was genuinely shocked. 'Who. . .who was your boyfriend?' he asked.

'Charles Hurst, of course. He didn't want any gossip, so we kept it quiet.'

'I see. Are you. . .still seeing him?'

She shook her head. 'No. It's all over now. He's got this job he's going to in London.'

'So you came up here?'

'Yes, I needed a change and—'

The thought came over her so suddenly, so sickeningly. At first she thought it ridiculous. But it wouldn't go away. Then she realised how well it would fit in. Charles must have suspected that he would be offered the job in London. He knew that if she started medical training she'd never accompany him. So. . .

It wasn't Neil who voted against her in the interview. It was Charles.

For a moment she felt sick, so great was her sense of betrayal. Her body swayed and Neil put out a steadying hand. She thought of asking him for details—but this was something between herself and Charles.

Hoarsely she said to Neil, 'I'd like to go back now.'

'Of course. Stay here in the cabin; it's still raining outside.'

Once again a detached part of her mind noted his

sensitivity. He obviously guessed what she'd guessed; knew what she was suffering. But he also knew that she didn't want sympathy. This was something she had to deal with herself.

She barely noticed the trip back to the marina, the short run to the car and the ride back. In no time they were back outside her little flat. He shook hands with her formally.

'I've enjoyed your company,' he said. 'I hope we can do it again and. . .everything goes well with you.'

She could appreciate what he was doing. 'Thank you,' she said. 'I thoroughly enjoyed—' the words stuck in her throat '—well, most of the night.'

He remained a minute longer on her doorstep and then went, saying nothing.

It wasn't too late. She rang Charles. She knew that he still had a week to go before he left for London. She was in luck; he was still in. 'Charles, this is Suzanne.'

He should have realised that something was wrong; as ever, he didn't. 'Hello. Don't tell me, you're tired of life in the frozen North and you want to come to London with me.'

Not for the first time she wondered what planet Charles came from. 'No,' she said through gritted teeth. 'Charles, my interview for medical school. Did you vote against me?' Part of her was still hoping that he'd say, no, certainly not. It was hard to contemplate such a betrayal from someone she'd been fond of.

'Well, you know, Zanne, I can't really be asked that kind of question. You know very well that. . .'

Sick at heart, she replaced the receiver. Charles was blustering. He *was* the one who voted against her.

It was too late to go for a walk, a swim or a run.

There was no one she could talk to. For some reason, she was nearly as angry at Neil as she was at Charles.

For an hour she sat by the fire, waiting for her anger—the pain of her betrayal—to ebb away. It didn't. For a while Charles had been part of her life. She'd thought she'd known him. To discover that he could be so treacherous—that she had been so wrong about him—made her question her own judgement. Could any man be trusted? She went to bed but it was dawn before she slept.

Next morning Sally O'Neill's husband arrived. Zanne took him to see his wife, and when she saw the way they flew into each other's arms she was torn apart with envy. There were arrangements to be made, and all three of them had to speak to Neil.

'Could I have a private word with you?' she asked Neil when it was convenient.

'There's an office here we can use.'

They sat, he behind the desk and she in a chair drawn up to it. Still cold, she thanked him again for the meal last night.

'I enjoyed it,' he replied. 'But if I had known how the evening would end I would never have invited you.'

'Thank you,' she said briefly. 'I phoned Charles Hurst last night. Now I know who voted against me in the interview. Just for once you can forget medical ethics and tell me exactly what happened.'

'Are you sure you want to know?'

'I need to know.'

He spoke in a precise, almost clinical voice as if reviewing a case. She had heard consultants using the same dry tone. They used it when discussing a case—

an amputation or when someone was sure to die—in which it was necessary to distance the entire group from emotional implications.

'The admission tutor and I had no doubts. We thought you were an admirable choice. I had been given the job of pushing you—of trying to make you feel uneasy. You coped with it very well. However, Hurst said he had worked with you on the ward and that you were careless, slipshod and had no great interest in the patients. But you were very persuasive, as we have just seen.'

She hadn't thought that she could have suffered more; now she knew differently.

'Why didn't you and Dr Dawkins have the courage of your convictions?' she managed to ask eventually.

'Dr Dawkins had told us that the decision had to be unanimous. He also said our discussions had to be confidential. Apparently there had been some trouble the year before over an embarrassing leak. Hurst convinced us, through his personal knowledge, that you weren't suitable. I can only say that I'm sorry.'

'Charles wanted me to go to London to live with him. He knew I wouldn't if I was accepted for medical training. So he lied about me to get his own way.'

His face looked stricken. 'All I can say is that I did what I thought was right and I'm sorry. But it's not enough, is it?'

'No. It's not enough.'

Walking out of the office, Zanne realised that Neil had acted properly, responsibly and ethically. Decisions were difficult; she would probably have done the same herself. But she still thought that she hated all men.

CHAPTER SEVEN

ZANNE hated all men. She knew that this was unfair but it was the way she felt. She made some excuse and blundered out of the office. She didn't even want Neil's restrained sympathy. She could do without men. It was the only way she could cope with the horror of what had happened to her.

She had only walked a few yards when she heard him call. 'Zanne, wait a minute.'

She turned, ready to tell him not to bother; that she didn't want to hear what he had to say. Then she heard him clearly. His voice was different, professional rather than personal.

'Sister Ripley, Dr Mitchell wants to talk to you.' It was the only thing that could have stopped her. She paused. 'He's on the phone now.'

Quickly she ran back to the office.

'It's Corporal Williams,' Alan said without preamble. 'Nick Cornish managed to call in this morning. The Corporal is as awkward as ever, but Nick thinks he's much worse. Could you manage to call in? I'd go myself, but I've got a visit with the midwife up to Black Ghyll and it's going to be a long trip.'

'I can go right now,' said Zanne. It was what she needed—something requiring her professional medical skills.

'I really appreciate it, Zanne. I know you'll do a good job.'

She could tell that Alan meant it, and the unexpected, only half-deliberate compliment did much to restore her self-esteem.

'It's what I do,' she said. For the moment it was the highest praise she could imagine anyone wanting.

'If there's any problem, then ring me. You understand, Zanne? Any problem at all.'

'I'll see that Corporal Williams gets the best of attention,' she said, and she half heard his acknowledgement of relief.

As she replaced the receiver she was unwelcomely reminded that she was not alone. 'I heard your conversation,' Neil said. 'Are you talking about that old soldier in Fenton woods?'

Zanne found that she could talk to Neil on medical matters. It made other concerns less important. 'He's possibly suffering from a respiratory infection,' she said. 'Dr Mitchell asked me to keep an eye on him.'

'I'll come with you.'

Her first reaction was to shout a violent no. But then she realised that she was a professional, engaged upon a professional task. She had no right to personal feelings.

'Your help would be welcome,' she said flatly.

'I'll bring a doctor's bag. What else?'

She thought. 'Bring a torch.'

They had to borrow a Land Rover from the hall, and explain where they were going. There was no problem; this was the kind of work John Brownlees was happy to help with. Twenty minutes later they were bumping along the track towards Fenton woods. It was easy to ignore Neil's presence as they drove, but harder as they walked up the dank path leading to the little hut.

'How did you know about the Corporal?' she asked

as they pushed aside fronds of wet bracken.

'The old soldier? I met him by chance in the woods. When you saw him was he wearing an old greatcoat with medal ribbons sewn on?'

'He was in bed. I saw the coat but I didn't notice any ribbons. Why? Are you an expert on medals, as well as everything else?'

He ignored her sharpness. 'I'm not an expert. But he had a medal ribbon that my grandfather had. And another I recognised. I told him this and that's how we got talking.'

'Which medals?' she asked, intrigued in spite of herself.

'One ribbon was yellow with a broad red central stripe and lesser stripes of light blue and dark blue. It was a Second World War Star—for fighting in Africa. That's what my grandfather had.'

'Go on.'

'The second was just a plain crimson ribbon.'

There was something about the way he said it that made her cautious. 'I'm afraid I don't know what that means.'

'Too many people don't. That's the ribbon of the Victoria Cross. Corporal Williams was a war hero.'

For a moment she felt ashamed of herself. But why? It was a long time ago. Her voice was sharp again. 'So you're another man fascinated by war and killing?'

He walked on a while before answering, and when he did his voice was thoughtful. 'No, Zanne, I'm not fascinated by war. I'm a doctor.' He paused and then went on, 'I was once in South America, in a region where there was a lot of guerilla warfare. I passed through a town where there'd been a bit of a battle—

just a few dozen people on each side. It had turned into a massacre. A priest got onto my train, asked if I was a doctor and, if so, could I spare two days of my life? I said I'd have a look.'

He climbed neatly over a ruined wall and turned to offer her a hand. She ignored it, and scrambled up herself. 'Go on,' she said.

'The priest had twenty-odd young men—and women—lying in his church. Mostly bullet and mortar wounds. They all looked alike; you couldn't tell which were government soldiers and which were guerillas. Well, I treated them as best I could, with equipment that should have been scrapped years ago. Don't tell the BMA but I performed a couple of operations. Scalpel in one hand and textbook in the other.'

She had to ask. 'Were you successful?'

He smiled sourly. 'Well, they were still alive when I left. The two days had stretched to ten. And I missed the climb I was heading for. No, Zanne, I'm not fascinated by war.'

They walked on in silence for a while longer, then she said, 'I'm being a bit of a pig to you, aren't I? And you're being good to me.'

He shook his head. 'Wounds to the soul are harder to heal than wounds to the body, Zanne. But time will help.'

The silence as they walked on was now more companionable. They weren't enemies any more. She realised that subconsciously she'd been trying to avoid thinking about him. Up to last night he had been the man who had stopped her becoming a doctor. All her feelings towards him were coloured by this one blazing fact. Now it turned out that he was innocent of the charge she'd laid against him. She felt guilty; she knew her feelings might alter. But for the moment she was shying away from this—it was too new, a bit frightening.

They came to the clearing with the derelict little barn. At first the day had been grey, then the occasional raindrop had pattered through the leaves but now it started to rain in earnest.

Neil pulled up the hood of his anorak. 'Corporal Williams lives here?' he asked in disbelief.

She nodded. 'He just won't be moved.'

'Hmm. I don't want to sound like a social worker but. . .'

'It's worse inside.'

There was no answer to their shouts, so they brushed aside the blanket and entered. 'Corporal Williams, it's me—Sister Ripley. Remember, I came with Dr Mitchell the other day?'

It was still dark, still damp, in the hut. There was no fire and she thought she heard a groan. Her nurse's nose twitched; she could tell that someone in here was ill.

Neil switched on his torch, illuminating the unwelcoming stone walls and earth floor. As before, there was a figure on the bed. It rolled over. Weakly a voice said, 'There's nothing wrong with me; go away.'

'I've brought Dr Calder to see you.'

Neil's voice was pleasant but firm. 'Good morning, Corporal. We met a couple of weeks ago in the woods.' He looked at the tins of food piled on the table. 'How long since you had breakfast?'

After a long pause, 'Not been feeling hungry,' came from the bed.

'We'll get you something now. Soup, I think.'

Neil turned to her, eyebrows raised. She nodded, looked at the table and winced. There was an ancient Primus stove and a couple of disreputable-looking pans. Perhaps she could manage to provide something.

The Primus needed pricking, and she had to run to the stream to rinse out the pans. But eventually there was a tin of Scotch broth coming up to the boil.

While she was busy she'd been listening to Neil and the corporal. Neil sat on the edge of the bunk and chatted. 'My grandfather was in the desert, you know; he was an artillery man. Commanded twenty-five-pounders at El Alamein.'

'Hmm. I was in the LRDG.'

'The Long Range Desert Group? Stirling's mob?'

The voice was still weak, but now showed some interest. 'You know about Stirling, then? Not many people care any more.'

'You're wrong there, Corporal; they do. Now, let me have a listen to your chest.'

Zanne knew what Neil was doing, and had to admire him. She'd heard doctors handling awkward patients before, but few were as skilful as this man. She realised, though, that Neil's interest wasn't feigned.

It took the two of them to ease the old man into a sitting position, and then she had to support him as Neil listened with his stethoscope. Corporal Williams was much, much weaker.

They managed to pack bedding behind the old man, and then she fed him the soup. He couldn't manage to hold the spoon himself. When he'd finished the tin he lapsed into a light sleep.

Neil beckoned her over. 'He's got to go to hospital.

He needs specialist care immediately. If he's not admitted in the next few hours he'll die. I've got my mobile phone here; I'll send for an ambulance.'

'How are we going to get him to the ambulance? He can't walk.'

'True.' He thought for a moment and then said, 'I saw Mike Deeley giving the trainees some practice on mountain rescue. They've got one of those mountain stretchers. They can come here and carry the corporal out. It'll be a good exercise for them.'

'Good idea. We'd better phone Alan Mitchell first. He's the corporal's official doctor.'

But it was impossible to raise Alan on his mobile phone. 'Black Ghyll's in a radio shadow,' Zanne said. 'I think he told me that before.'

'We'll go ahead anyhow. We daren't waste time.'

It was the kind of medical emergency that could only happen in the country, and everyone worked well together. John Brownlees got Mike to set off with the stretcher and eight good trainees. The receptionist at Alan's surgery alerted the hospital and organised the ambulance to rendezvous at the bottom of the forestry track. The only problem was persuading Corporal Williams.

He woke after a while and, after drinking the tea Zanne had made, pronounced himself much better. 'You may go now,' he said. 'All I need is rest.'

'We've sent for the ambulance,' Neil said. 'I'm afraid it's a short stay in hospital.'

'Not for me, thank you.' The corporal lay down and pulled the tattered blankets about him defensively.

'Corporal, when you were on patrol did anyone get shot—wounded by the Germans?'

'Yes. One or two.'

'And you left them behind to be picked up by the Germans?'

'Certainly not! We carried our men back.'

'Well, that's what we're going to do with you. We're carrying you back.'

'I am staying here.'

'Corporal Williams, you will go back in the ambulance and that is an order!' The shouted order echoed round the little hut, and Zanne jerked with shock. You didn't talk to patients like that!

But it worked. For a moment the old man and the doctor stared at each other. Then there was a mumbled, 'Yessir,' and the corporal's eyes closed. Neil stooped to take his pulse for a moment, and then moved over to join Zanne in the doorway.

'I like your bedside manner,' she laughed. 'But I can think of consultants who wouldn't approve.'

'It worked. In fact, the old man wanted to be bullied. He knows he's got to go to hospital.'

'I see.' Once again she was surprised by the shrewdness of this man. He knew about people—for a doctor it was just as important as knowing about illness. 'Will he be all right?'

'I think so, yes. In some ways he lives quite a reasonable life. He's organically sound. But he shouldn't come back here.'

Together they watched the rain hissing down. 'This is a bit different from practising medicine in hospital,' she said.

'True, but I like it. Hospitals are fine but you're cocooned from life. 'I've practised medicine. . .' With a laugh, he corrected himself, 'Well, I've *tried* to act like a doctor in a lot of weird places. In tents often enough, and once even in an ice cave. This hut may be a bit primitive but there's no heat to make infection worse. No insects, and the only poisonous snakes are adders. Friendly, compared to some snakes I've met.'

'We had an adder bite in Casualty two years ago,' Zanne said. 'A little girl walking in the woods trod on one. She was all right after twenty-four hours and went back to school to be a heroine.'

'Hmm. In the jungle in Borneo I came across a King cobra on a trail once. With an erect hood. I just stood still and after a while it slipped away.'

'How big?' Zanne asked, shuddering.

'About four feet long.'

'And you had the presence of mind just to stand still?'

He grinned. 'Well, that's one interpretation. The other is that I was too terrified to move. Is that Mike's party I can hear?'

While he went out to meet them she slipped back to prepare the corporal. She quite liked talking to Neil. And while she was kept busy she hadn't thought about Charles Hurst at all. The feeling of sickness—of betrayal—came back but it wasn't as violent as it had been before.

Mike came into the clearing at the head of his little group. Zanne was pleased to see that there were two girls in the group of eight. She'd had her differences with Mike before but here he was assured and efficient, deferring to Neil's superior medical knowledge.

Carefully, she and Neil transferred the old man to the stretcher. He was well wrapped, and Zanne saw to the waterproof cover and the straps that would ensure

that he didn't slip. Corporal Williams now seemed to
have accepted his fate. But just before the trainees came
in to pick him up he pulled her head down towards
him. 'That square stone in the corner,' he muttered,
pointing cautiously. 'It's behind that square stone in the
corner. Get him to keep them. I don't trust hospitals.'

She waited until the stretcher had been carefully
carried out and then went to the stone he had indicated.
It was loose, and behind it was an old tin. She
recognised it as the kind used in the last war to send
cigarettes to troops.

'What have you got there?' Neil had appeared
behind her.

'He wants you to keep it for him.' She proffered
the tin.

He opened it. Inside was a cloth, and wrapped in it
was a row of medals. He pointed to one with a crimson
ribbon attached—a bronze cross with the words FOR
VALOUR in the centre.

'The Victoria Cross,' he said. He turned the medal
to study the name and date on the back. 'The British
army's highest award for bravery. Quite a man in his
time was Corporal Williams.' He put the tin carefully
in his anorak pocket.

It wasn't easy walking down the path with the heavy
stretcher. Neil or Zanne tried to keep to the side of the
old man to check on his condition. Mike changed the
stretcher-bearers frequently, and ranged ahead looking
for the easiest route. And the rain sluiced down
on them.

Once they were on the hard forestry path things
were easier. They saw the ambulance ahead, and two
paramedics came to meet them. In no time, it seemed

Corporal Williams was transferred to the gurney and
the ambulance was driving away.

'A job well done, lads—and lasses,' Neil said cheerfully. 'This wasn't an exercise; it was the real thing.'

'Now get back in the Land Rover,' Mike added. 'The
day's not over yet. We'll go and practise using the
stretcher on the rock face.'

He smiled at the chorus of groans. Then he bit his
lip. 'Neil, I'm sorry, I forgot. Message for you.' He
gave Zanne a sly look. 'There's a go-o-orgeous blonde
waiting for you at the hall. And she's French!
Mam'selle de Courcy?'

'Claudette!' shouted Neil, obviously delighted.

Zanne wondered why she felt dispirited.

'Zanne, this is Claudette de Courcy. We have slept
with each other on many occasions. Claudette—Zanne
Ripley.' It was an unusual introduction and Zanne
blinked with surprise.

The tall, elegant woman standing next to Neil
jammed her elbow hard into his ribs. Neil gasped. 'Neil,
you mus' not tease,' she scolded. Then she smiled and
extended her hand. 'Miss Ripley—Zanne—I am mos'
happy to make your acquaintance.'

Zanne was a little overwhelmed. Claudette was a bit
older than she, perhaps in her mid-thirties. She was
slim and svelte, dressed in an obviously expensive grey
silk suit. On her lapel was a tiny golden brooch in the
form of a cat.

'Let's sit down,' Neil suggested and ushered them
towards seats in the lounge. It was then that Zanne
noticed. There was something about the way that
Claudette moved that she recognised. It was not the

hobble of a fashion-plate from the Rue St Honoré. The stride was too long, the body movement too controlled. Then it struck her. 'You're Claudette le Chat!' she cried.

Everyone who read climbing magazines knew of Claudette le Chat. She climbed alone—usually without ropes—tackling some of the hardest rock faces in the world. Zanne had seen films of her, and had marvelled and flinched at what she was doing.

'You are very kin'. And, yes, I have slept many times with Neil. But always with our clothes on—in a tent or a hut. One time in an ice cave. You're a climber, so you know. But he is wrong to tease his fiancée.'

'I'm not his fiancée,' Zanne said crisply, and was annoyed when she caught the look of derision on Neil's face.

'Ah, I am sorry. I just thought. . .'

What Claudette thought Zanne never discovered. Neil put in, 'Claudette's just here till tomorrow morning. She needs to talk to me. We're going down to the Stag's Head for a quick meal later on. Why don't you come down after surgery and have a drink with us? Nothing exciting, just a low-pressure meeting of friends.'

She would have loved to talk to Claudette. But they were old friends; they needed to be left together. 'You'll have things to talk about,' she said. 'You don't want me.'

However, they both pressed her to come. And reluctantly—or happily—she agreed that she would.

For the second time in two days Zanne found herself wondering about what clothes to wear when she went out for a drink with Neil Calder. But after the heartache of the day before she decided that she wasn't going to anything like as much trouble.

And how *did* she now feel? Still angry, still bitter, still betrayed. When she thought that she'd once been quite fond of Charles Hurst she shuddered. And it was wrong to take out her anger on Neil Calder, who had, she supposed, acted quite properly. Still, he could have given her a hint.

In the end she wore what was the hall undress uniform, a tracksuit with an anorak thrown over the top. And it was quite easy to get a lift down to the pub.

She found the two deep in conversation in a corner. Their table was scattered with photographs, and Claudette was writing intently in a notebook. They didn't see her. Zanne asked the barman what the two were drinking and bought another red wine and a beer. For herself she had the usual white wine. Then she walked over.

'You're obviously not finished,' she said, putting down the drinks. 'I want to listen while you talk.'

'Good idea,' Neil mumbled, reaching for his drink. 'Now, Claudette, this is the crux.' He took up a photograph and pointed. 'You've got to commit early because you'll be very tired. There's a good handhold here, although it's not obvious. Once you've made the move you can't go back. But afterwards it's all straightforward.'

'I see.' Claudette scribbled more in her notebook. 'That is all, I think, Neil. Now it is up to me.'

Neil fanned the photographs out and showed them to Zanne. 'This is a four-hundred-foot climb I did in the Dolomites. I was the first to do it; no one's done it since. Now Claudette wants to try so she came to me for advice.'

Zanne flinched as she looked at the photographs. She herself was quite a competent rock-climber. But this route was far far harder than anything she'd ever dream of attempting. 'A lot of climbers would try to protect their climb,' she said. 'Won't you mind if Claudette manages it?'

He shook his head. 'Someone will do it in time. I'd like it if that someone was Claudette.'

The rest of the evening was spent in general casual talk about climbing. Later on a couple of others from the hall joined them; the pub was almost their club. Then Neil drove them back and dropped her off outside her flat.

As Neil had promised, it had been a low-pressure evening. After the previous night it was what Zanne needed—she almost suspected that Neil knew this. She went to bed early and dropped instantly into a dreamless sleep.

Next morning Claudette and Neil called briefly on her to say goodbye. Claudette was flying back to France, and Neil was going to London for a week. In a way she wasn't sorry to see them go. She felt that she needed time to herself. For the rest of the morning she worked on autopilot. In her free hours in the afternoon she decided to go for a solitary walk.

For an hour she maintained a hard, fast pace up Fenton Fell, moving steadily upwards and concentrating solely on the route. Eventually she reached the little outcrop on the top of the fell, and sat to eat an apple.

Now, while the blood was still rushing round her body, was a good time to think.

First, Charles's betrayal. She'd known about it for less than forty-eight hours. The sheer disbelief was still with her—how could any man do such a thing? The pain was still there but perhaps it was receding. She could apply for medical school again next year. Perhaps try different medical schools. She had to be resilient. And it was good to know that she'd convinced two people of her merit—Dr Dawkins and Neil.

Now Neil. She thought that she could forgive him for sticking to his principles and not telling her about the interview. She chuckled to herself. The way she'd treated him, he must have been very tempted at times.

She had no cause to dislike him any more. And she was attracted to him. She knew that he was attracted to her—so what next? She felt wary. He was a man and she'd just been bitterly let down by a man. Perhaps she should think solely of her career.

An affair with Neil would be no milk-and-water affair, such as she'd had with Charles. It would be real, passionate. But it would also be short. Claudette would not *be* a rival for Zanne—what Claudette *represented* was the rival. Neil had wanderlust. She couldn't, wouldn't, want to tame it. But she wanted a permanent relationship. And she didn't want one with a man who was away for nine months of the year.

'Of course, he just might not want anything from me at all,' she muttered. Then she walked back to the hall.

Ward 17. It was good to be back, just for a while. She stood unnoticed, watched the scurrying student nurses and savouring that evocative smell of floor polish and disinfectant. She had only been away for six weeks and she loved her work at Lawiston Hall, but she realised that this place would always be part of her.

She tiptoed over and peered through the open office door. Her friend, Mary Kelly, was bent over the desk, trying to cope with the interminable bookwork.

'Since you're getting married tomorrow I think you should take the rest of the day off,' Zanne said mischievously.

'Zanne! We didn't expect you till tonight!' Zanne was enfolded in a bear hug. 'It's good to see you. And you're looking so fit and brown!'

'I'm looking forward to. . .'

There was a tap on the door and a worried-looking student nurse peered in. 'Sister, it's Mr Ralston. He's gone all red-faced and he's gasping for breath and I can't. . .'

Mary sighed. 'All right, Nurse Dixon, it's another anxiety attack; he's had them before. I'll come and show you what to do.' She looked glumly at the pile of papers on her desk. 'I suppose I can do these later.'

Zanne pressed her back into her seat. 'Lend me a white coat,' she coaxed. 'I'll show Nurse Dixon how it's done.'

Mary's eyes sparkled. 'Free help!' she said. 'And competent, too. Take one of those coats off the back of the door.'

It was quite a bad attack and Zanne wanted the student nurse to understand why things had to be done, as well as how to do them. Eventually, after reassuring the distressed man, they had him breathing into a paper bag, and slowly he calmed down. They stayed with

him for a while, and so it was three-quarters of an hour
before Zanne could get back to Mary to drink coffee
and pick up on the gossip. It was good to be back in
harness again.

It was a quiet registry office wedding, with Zanne as
maid of honour and only a handful of guests. Both
Mary and her fiancé, Robert, had been married before
and they didn't want too much ostentation. They both
had children, too, who seemed to be getting on very
well with each other. Zanne thought that everything
seemed to be working out satisfactorily. She wondered
if ultimately she would do as well.

The big reception and party took place that night in
the Belham Hall Hotel. Zanne got there early, stood in
the middle of the empty ballroom and was affected by
memories. This was where she had argued with Neil,
where Peter Collins had fallen off the balcony and
where she'd taken off her dress. And what had
happened since then?

She shook herself irritably. She was too young to be
affected by the past—she had the future to look forward
to. What future? At the moment it looked—well, it
was impossible to tell.

Then old friends from the hospital turned up and she
cast aside such thoughts.

It was a good party with a good disco. Mary was
popular and her friends were Zanne's friends. Zanne
talked and danced as if there were no tomorrow, and
ate and drank in moderation. She was enjoying herself.
And then, near midnight—just when Cinderella should
have left the ball—she heard a voice behind her say,
'D'you think you would dance with me?'

There was a sense of inevitability about it. Neil had gone to London a week ago; there was no reason why he should turn up here. But he had done, and she didn't feel at all surprised. She wondered why.

She turned. 'What are you doing here?'

He took her unresisting hand and led her onto the floor. 'I'm still working for the medical school, remember? I had some results to collate; people to see.'

The music started, a slow, moody song by Frank Sinatra. Neil slipped his hand round Zanne's waist and guided her gently. 'I heard about this do and that you'd be here so I wangled an invitation.'

'What? Just to see me?' she asked pertly. 'I'm honoured, sir.'

'I wanted to see you as a person again, not as a nurse. Somewhere where we didn't have to act as professionals.'

'There's somebody about to fall off the balcony,' she said, and giggled when he jerked round to look.

'Sometimes you're a devil.' He tightened his hold on her, his body moulded to hers. She could feel the line of his thigh, and the muscles of his chest and shoulder.

She said nothing more. For a while she was content to be held and to move in time to the music, eyes half-closed. Close to, she could smell him—the hint of an expensive cologne and underneath the exciting scent of male warmth.

The dance ended; the lights came on. She released him reluctantly; she'd been blissfully happy in his arms. But things were happening.

Mary and her new husband were leaving. First they had to come to the centre of the floor for the shortest

of speeches. They were liberally showered with con-
fetti. Then the entire party surged into the car park to
watch them drive away. The car, of course, had been
decorated. It disappeared to the sound of rattling tins
tied to the bumper.

'All medical parties are good,' Neil said as they
returned. 'I've never been to an unenthusiastic one yet.'

'It's because we're often close to death,' she said.
'It makes living more valuable.'

'That's very perceptive,' he said thoughtfully.

'Come and tell us what your new job's like, Zanne.'
She was beckoned to join yet another group. It seemed
natural that Neil should go with her.

The party was more relaxed now. There was less
dancing and more sitting and talking. Neil seemed content to sit and listen, as long as he could sit next to
her. Then George Dent, husband of the sister on Ward
23, heard that he had been to South America.

'I'd love to go there,' he said eagerly. 'Did you see
any birds?'

Zanne tried to hide her smile. She'd listened to many
a complaint about how George was interested in one
thing only—bird-watching!

'Well, I upset a condor when I was climbing,' Neil
said. 'It attacked me.'

George couldn't have been more excited. 'A condor!
How I'd love to see a condor! How close to it did
you get?'

'Too close. I was climbing this very wet bit of rock
face. Obviously the condor thought it was his bit of
territory so it tried to frighten me off. It frightened me
all right—they have an eight-foot wingspan, you know.

Look like dragons. Unfortunately I couldn't fly away. But I nearly fell off.'

He apparently didn't realise that the rest of the table had fallen silent, as engrossed in his story as George was.

'I believe condors are very territorial,' George went on excitedly. 'Did you. . .'

But his wife had had enough of birds for one night. 'I want to dance, George,' she said. 'Come on.'

'But. . .' There were no buts. George was led away.

'I'd like to dance as well,' Zanne said, and she too was led onto the floor.

It was a good party but soon it was time to leave. Neil waited as Zanne picked up her coat from the cloakroom. 'How are you getting home?' he asked. 'For that matter, where are you staying?'

'I'm staying at Mary Kelly's house and I'm sharing a taxi back with her two kids,' Zanne explained. 'It was all worked out before.' She waved to the two friendly teenagers who were saying goodbye to their own little group.

'I see. Goodnight, then, Zanne.' He gave her the briefest of kisses and walked away.

Sitting in the taxi, she wondered about the evening. She agreed with the children that Mary's send-off had been fabulous. They'd all enjoyed themselves.

On a personal level, she wondered how her relationship with Neil had progressed. He had deliberately sought her out, contriving an invitation to the party. But once he had her company he'd been content to keep things low key. Was he being casual—or confident?

CHAPTER EIGHT

AS ARRANGED, Zanne slept the night in Mary Kelly's bed. And at half past eight in the morning the telephone rang. She knew who it was before she picked up the receiver. Why was Neil phoning her?

A laughing voice said, 'Good morning! Who's still asleep?'

'What d'you want?' she asked gracelessly. 'Don't you know what time it is?'

'It's getting-up time. And you've got the voice of a girl with hair over her face, and pink and white striped pyjamas. We doctors can tell these things.'

'My hair's in a plait and I'm wearing a red flannel nightie—look, what's it got to do with you what I wear in bed?'

'At the moment, nothing—but a man can dream.'

She was waking up properly now and she blushed as she considered this remark and its implications.

'Why I really phoned is that I'm driving back to Lawiston Hall this afternoon. I thought you might like to travel with me.'

She thought for a moment. She wasn't actually due back at the hall until tomorrow morning, but the offer of a lift would save her time and trouble. 'That's kind of you,' she said slowly. 'Yes, I'd like a lift.'

'Good. Shall I pick you up there?'

'No, I'm visiting the hospital this morning. How about meeting in the staff car park?'

142

'See you there at two.' He rang off.

She couldn't get back to sleep so she lay in bed and considered. Half of her didn't want to spend so much time with him until she'd got her feelings for him sorted out. The other half of her knew very well that she was looking forward to the trip. She sighed, and climbed out of bed.

At two o'clock she walked over to the staff car park, her bag slung easily over her shoulder. He was already waiting for her. 'I like towns,' he said as they cruised through the suburbs, 'but I like leaving them as well.'

'So you're affected by wanderlust even when you're just driving down the road?' she asked, a touch sourly.

'Afraid so. The lure of the open road.' He slowed because of a giant lorry ahead. 'Or as open as the road ever is in England.'

She decided to stick to safe subjects for a while. 'What were you doing in London?' she asked. 'How's your research coming along?'

He shrugged. 'As with all research these days, there's an awful lot of material that's already available. You've just got to find it. I've been doing a lot of boring statistical work on the computer. There are a lot of facts available from America—people's lives seem to be more quantified and filed than ours are. We now think we know some of the factors that go to producing long life.'

'Well, that's a start.'

'Possibly. We're trying ultimately to find out how to make people live longer. I'm not sure that we shouldn't concentrate on ensuring that they enjoy the time they have.'

'That's why you're interested in endorphins. Would you try to synthesise them? So you could give people a pill that made them happy and yet was entirely safe?'

'Good Lord, no!' he said, obviously revolted at the idea.

'Why not? I know why. You think happiness should be worked for—as by exercise. Dr Calder, you're a Puritan at heart, just like me.'

'Are you a puritan, Nurse Ripley? With a deep-seated distrust of all the pleasures of the flesh?'

'My deep-seated distrust is of young men who try to introduce me to the pleasures of the flesh,' she said demurely. 'But I do like some. For instance, I'm very fond of coffee.'

'The Lord protect me from smart women,' he muttered, but smiled as he said it.

They drove for a few miles in companionable silence. By now they were on the motorway and, as ever, she was waiting for the first dim line of hills to show on the horizon.

'My heart always jumps when I see them,' she explained to Neil. 'It's as if something is about to start. You get the same feeling when you drive into Wales and see Snowdon in the distance.'

'I know what you mean,' he agreed. 'You've just got to go. I've felt it driving up from India. It's flat, hot and dusty. Then, suddenly, there are the Himalayas.'

'All right, all right,' she protested. 'I'm upstaged. I'm just an ignorant provincial. The nearest I've been to the Himalayas is in the local cinema.'

'Sorry,' he said. 'Didn't mean to be like that. Honestly. My old headmaster used to say that travel lengthens the tongue without broadening the mind. That's what happened to me.'

He reached over to pat her hand, then held it gently. She sat in silence until he had to remove it to turn a corner. Then he took her hand again.

Suddenly she felt that she had to speak. She didn't know how, but their silence had passed from being friendly to something more meaningful. 'I enjoyed the party last night,' she said in a falsely bright tone. 'Mary's a wonderful woman and Robert is just the man for her. It's the second time for both of them. And I know Mary had resigned herself to remaining a widow.'

'There's always time for love, Zanne,' he said sombrely. 'Always time for love.'

Now, what did he mean by that? she brooded.

They had now turned off the motorway and were travelling along a main road. He slowed and turned right onto a much smaller road. 'Where are we going?' she asked. This was the beginning of the Lake District, an attractive area but not one she knew well.

'I thought you might like a cup of tea,' he said. 'A sandwich, even.'

'Y-e-s,' she said slowly. 'D'you know of a pub or restaurant or something?'

'I know all of those round here,' he said enigmatically, but would not be drawn further.

They came to a tiny village called Thraken—just a handful of grey stone cottages. Neil sounded his hooter and waved at an old man who was working in a beautifully kept garden. Then he turned right, down a gravel drive.

They pulled up at the front of a house and Zanne looked about her, delighted. The house was built of the local green-grey stone and slate. It was old—probably mid-Victorian. Behind was a curtain of trees and in front there was a rocky, flower-strewn slope to a tiny tarn.

'It's beautiful,' Zanne exclaimed. 'Who lives here?'

'Well, if I ever stop wandering,' he said, 'then I will.'

For a while the two of them sat in the car. When she'd looked round, she glanced at him. His eyes were fixed on the trees, and held an expression she'd never seen before. There was a calmness, a satisfaction with what he surveyed. He felt her regard and turned towards her. 'Would you like to look inside?' he asked.

Of course she would. But as she stepped out of the car she felt that she was taking the first step towards an unknown future.

It didn't smell musty or unlived-in inside; in fact, there was the faint smell of woodsmoke. Neil explained that old Jake at the end looked after the garden and his wife kept an eye on the house. 'I phoned her this morning and asked her to light a fire. Sit down while I make us some tea.'

He took her to the living-room and sat her in a chintz seat by a slate fireplace where logs smoked. As soon as he'd left the room she jumped up; she couldn't sit still. She had to inspect the room.

It was comfortable, cheerful, lived-in. There were windows on three sides, each with a wonderful view. There was a piano with music on its top, bookshelves and framed photographs.

A recent photograph was obviously of Neil's family. There were his parents, a brother looking quite like him and a wife and children. Zanne saw that Neil got his sometimes fierce handsomeness from his father;

his mother looked much more gentle.

Another photograph showed Neil on top of some icy peak; he had full climber's gear and a beard. She thought he looked quite piratical. Another photograph showed him as a teenager in shorts and singlet, winning a race. She recognised the determined expression—he still had it.

Then the books—mostly medical and travel. She saw that he liked to annotate his reading; there were neatly written comments in the margins. 'Try further to the left,' he put by a description of a climb. And, 'Rubbish!' he'd written by another description. She smiled. He was always forthright.

'Are you making yourself at home?' There was a rattle as he entered with a tea-tray.

'It's a homely house,' she said. 'Anybody would be comfortable here. Is it your parents' house?'

He sat and poured tea. 'They've handed it over to me. What I'll do with it I don't know. It's the house I grew up in but I still love it. When you've finished your tea we'll have a look round.'

There was none of the dampness or chill associated with many Lakeland houses. His mother had insisted on unobtrusive double glazing; there was a powerful central heating system and Zanne fell for the Aga-centred kitchen at once. He showed her the study and the more formal dining-room. Then they went upstairs.

'This was—is—my bedroom,' he said. She looked round, fascinated. The books, the pictures, the collection of rocks, all hinted at the man he was to become.

'Now, come and lie on the bed.'

'Come and what?' she demanded. She couldn't believe what she'd heard.

'Come and lie on the bed,' he said sardonically. 'What did you think I had in mind? Good Lord, Zanne, give me credit for some sensitivity.'

'Sorry,' she said, and lay down as he indicated.

'Now, you're a seven-year-old with rheumatic fever. You're too ill to do anything—watch television, listen to the radio or read—which is what you do most. Friends and family come in to visit you—but you're usually glad when they go. Turn your head and look out of the window.'

When she did he asked, 'Now, what can you see?'

'There are the trees outside. And the top of the hill opposite—and in the distance I can see the blue outline of a mountain ridge.'

'That blue mountain ridge. For six weeks, Zanne, I stared at that ridge. I thought I'd never be well again, but if I was I was going to climb that mountain. It became a symbol to me of everything that I wanted and couldn't have.'

He held out his hand and pulled her off the bed. 'Sometimes I think that the sight of that ridge started me wandering.'

'Did you ever go there?'

'Oh, yes. I got my father to take me, and it was as wonderful as I'd thought it would be. The trouble is that I keep on seeing another ridge. And I'm not content till I go there.'

She knew that she'd have to think about the story. 'Can we look round outside now?' she asked abruptly.

There was the garden round the house, which Jake looked after, but there were also three or four acres of rough land which were left unattended. He took her round them, reminiscing happily. This was where a kingfisher once nested. This was where deer sometimes came to eat the young shoots. This was where he fell through the ice in the little tarn. Zanne shuddered at that story. They came back down the drive, and stopped for a chat with Jake.

It was getting dark as they neared the house again. He said, 'We can hurry back to the hall if you like. But, if you want, we can stay a little longer and I'll cook tea.'

He saw her pause. 'Don't let me persuade you. We'll have a coffee while you're thinking about it.'

She thought—hard—as he went to the kitchen. The uncomplicated thing to do would be to go back to the hall. If she stayed she'd risk—well, complications. Perhaps she ought to go back. But, even as she wondered, she knew that she would not.

'I'd like to stay for tea,' she said as he came in with the coffee. Then she searched his face, looking for some hint of triumph.

There was none. 'I'm very pleased,' he said. 'I like to spend time here when I can.'

He made up the fire and told her he didn't want any help in the kitchen. Zanne discovered that she was tired. She put her feet up on the fender and dozed.

An hour later Neil called her. She blinked; she'd slept more deeply than she'd realised. He suggested that she washed her face in the little downstairs cloakroom. Then they would eat in the dining-room.

She blinked again as he led her into the dining-room. The mahogany table was laid for two, with gleaming glasses, silver cutlery and white starched napkins. The sole light came from two candelabra.

'Sorry about the pretentiousness,' he said wryly. 'I seem to have spent a lot of my life eating out of tins in tents, or sandwiches while I'm working. So every now and again I like to indulge in a little gracious living.'

'Don't apologise,' she said faintly and then looked at him more closely. 'You've changed!' Instead of the jeans and sweater he was dressed in a white shirt and dark trousers.

'Well I. . .'

'Well, you can wait till I get my case out of the car and put a dress on!' Then she said anxiously, 'Ten minutes won't spoil anything, will it?'

'In fact I've allowed a quarter of an hour for us to have a sherry.'

'You should have told me.' She fled out to the car.

Fourteen minutes later she'd had the fastest shower of her life, pulled on the traditional little black dress and managed to do something with lipstick and mascara. She went downstairs.

'I'm not going to compliment you,' he said. 'You look lovely in whatever you wear.'

'Thank you, kind sir. Smooth talking will get you anywhere.' She let him seat her and pour her a sherry. She was glad that she'd changed; she felt that this was an occasion and she wanted to dress accordingly.

Zanne might have guessed—he was an excellent cook. He served chicken breasts in white wine with bacon and mushrooms, braised leeks and rice. Afterwards there was home-made ice cream and local cheese. They drank a bottle of his favourite Loire wine.

And they talked. He told her of practising medicine in hot, cold and just plain nasty climates. She told him

of her wish to be a doctor; of her mother's near-fatal
accident before she could start, and of her decision to
train as a nurse.

Afterwards they opened another bottle of Saumur
and sat together on the couch by the fire. She kissed
him first. 'Thank you for that wonderful meal,' she said.

'Just a little thing I whipped together from the
freezer. But it was home-made to start with.' He kissed
her back.

At first his kiss was diffident, a soft tasting of her
lips. She knew that if she wished to she could push
him away. In fact, her hand splayed open on his chest.
She could feel the warmth of his body, the rasp of the
hair against the fine cotton of his shirt. Underneath was
the pounding of his heart. It only kept pace with her
own accelerating pulse.

She moved her hand so that it circled under his arm,
grazing his nipple. She heard the tiny intake of his
breath. She half sat, half lay there, perfectly comfortable, waiting for what would happen next and knowing
that she was committed to a course from which there
would be no turning back.

He turned her so that her back was to him and pulled
her close. His hands caressed her waist, her hands holding the back of his. Her head was on his shoulder. He
kissed the side of her face, then her neck and gently
bit her ear. She thought she had never experienced such
bliss; her body was languorous, floating. Nothing was
too overwhelming; there was no danger—yet.

Somehow, the front of her dress had come undone.
His hand moved delicately down inside it, giving her
every opportunity to stop him. She didn't want to, thrill-
ing as his hand cupped her breasts. She took delight,

not only in the fire of her own feelings but also in the knowledge of the pleasure she was bringing him.

Gently, reluctantly, he released her. His voice was hoarse, vibrant with passion. 'I want you, Zanne, my darling. I want to love you. Will you come to bed with me?'

This was her last chance to change her mind, an offer generously given. She stood, and slipped off the black dress. 'I want to love you, too,' she said.

Taking his outstretched hand, she followed him upstairs. The click as the light was switched off seemed to echo round the room.

They went, inevitably, to his bedroom. She was glad. If she was to give herself to him she wanted it to be in this room, where he had become what he was.

It was a clear night so there was starlight through the window to see by. First he undressed her fully, pressing his lips on each part of her revealed body. Then he too undressed and came to lie by her side.

The touch of his hands as they ranged over her body brought her delight beyond anything she'd experienced before. Soon she was calling to him, asking him to love her fully.

Then his arms were round her, his body poised above hers. There was one fleeting moment of apprehension and an instant of pain. Then they were together, and the waves of ecstasy beat against her until she screamed aloud her fulfilment. 'I love you, my darling,' he sighed.

She slept well in his bedroom. After the emotional turmoil and physical rapture her body needed complete oblivion. She was happy when she woke in the morning. Beside her was the warm body of the man she loved. When she moved closer to him still asleep, he threw his arm around her. She felt a great surge of contentment. She loved him. She loved Neil Calder.

At last she admitted it to herself, and in the honesty of that admission there was a feeling of relief. She lay there without moving, awake and content in just being with him. She knew that whatever else happened to her or to them this was a moment of pure happiness she would always remember.

Slowly the darkness outside grew light. She could see the view that he so often must have seen. First the dimmest of outlines, then the sun hit the far distant peak. She knew what he meant—it was beautiful. It filled her, too, with the urge to travel—to wander.

As the light filled his room her eyes flicked round the sights that he so often must have seen—the books, the pictures, the mementoes. In a sense they now belonged to her, too.

But it was the room of a wanderer. Gradually the realisation grew of what this meant. He might love her, as much as he could love any woman. But there would always be another love—the lust to cross the horizon. And after every horizon there was always another. This was a love she could not compete with.

When she felt him beginning to stir she eased herself out of bed. She thought it was the hardest thing she had ever done.

'Come back here, Zanne,' his sleepy voice called out. 'I want an early morning kiss—or something.'

Deliberately she put on a bright, practical tone. 'Breakfast-time, sleepy-head. You stay there a minute.'

She found a dressing-gown behind his door, went

down and rooted round his kitchen. She made coffee the way she knew he liked it, and took two cups up to the bedroom. Outside the bedroom she stopped, then put one cup on the floor. If she took in two cups she'd get into bed, and if she got into bed. . . So she hastily took in his cup and put it on his bedside cabinet. 'Come down for breakfast in fifteen minutes,' she said, and ran before waiting for his reply.

She drank her coffee, made toast and fried bacon and eggs. The smell drifted round the house and after ten minutes he came down, dressed in an old tracksuit. He put his arms round her from behind and kissed the back of her neck. The spatula in her hand trembled.

'You don't have to prove you're wonderful—I know,' he whispered.

'Sit down,' she ordered, moving away from his embrace. 'Just for once I'm pretending that I'm domesticated and doing woman's work.'

'But I thought we might. . .'

'Breakfast,' she shouted, waving her spatula at him.

He took his place at the kitchen table. 'Well, perhaps I need my strength kept up,' he said slyly, and she blushed. Then she found refuge in practicalities.

'We both need to be back at Lawiston quite early,' she said.

He looked gloomy. 'I suppose so.'

After breakfast she made to clear away the dishes, but he put his hand across the table and stopped her. 'There's something I've got for you,' he said. 'I've been waiting for the right moment to give it to you. Perhaps this is it.'

There was an intensity in his eyes as he pushed a letter over the table towards her. She opened it.

Like letters she'd had before, it was headed 'University of the North, Department of Medicine. From the Office of the Tutor of Admissions.' But it wasn't the usual duplicated letter.

The letter explained that Dr Dawkins had been very impressed by her performance at her interview. Since he had sent her the letter of rejection, certain circumstances had changed. He regretted the undoubted disappointment she must have felt but, if she was still interested, he could offer her a place in medical school to start next September. Could she please let him have her decision within the next two weeks?

Her head was spinning; she could do nothing but sit there. She read the letter again and again, and turned it over to see if there was anything on the other side.

'I thought you'd be pleased,' he said anxiously.

'Oh Neil, I am, I am! It's what I wanted.' Some of her former confidence returned. 'And I think it's what I deserve. But how...why... Did you have anything to do with this?'

'Professional confidences,' he said smoothly. 'Medical etiquette prohibits me from saying.'

'It was you, I know! And I don't care what rules you've broken or how you've done it. I'm just glad.'

She ran round the table and kissed him. But it was a different sort of kiss from the night before. And she just couldn't contain her excitement or curiosity. 'Just what did you do?' she asked.

He frowned. 'I told the tutor of admissions exactly what you told me about Charles Hurst. I said I thought we'd both been deceived and that you had been injured. He made a few enquiries and decided on this course of action.' For a moment there was something wolfish in his expression. 'And the next time Charles applies for promotion, this matter will be brought up.'

Well, perhaps she should—but she was *not* going to feel sorry for Charles.

She started stacking dishes in the sink. 'Come on, Neil,' she said, 'we have to go. We don't want people talking. We're due back in Lawiston soon.'

'I suppose you're right. Look, Zanne, about last night. . .'

'Last night was gorgeous and you're a wonderful lover,' she said, too brightly. 'But now it's another day and we've both got work to do.'

He looked disappointed. 'It might be another day, but last night was something I'll never forget.'

'I'm sure I won't either,' she said, again in her over-bright voice. 'But let's not make too much of it. I'm going to train to be a doctor, and you'll be off on your travels again soon—won't you?'

'I suppose so,' he said heavily.

'I'm sure we'll meet; we'll keep in touch. After all, I'll be training in the same medical school you're researching in.'

'True.' He grabbed her, his face intense. 'Zanne, I think you're trying to tell me something, but I'm damned if I know what it is.'

It took all the strength she had to persist in her deception. 'What I'm telling you is that we have to be out of here in the next fifteen minutes.' She kissed him quickly. 'Now, move, man, move!'

A quarter of an hour later the Jaguar pulled out of the drive. Zanne hoped that he'd never know just what pain the last hour had cost her.

CHAPTER NINE

THE journey back to Lawiston Hall started silently and Zanne was pleased when Neil pushed in a tape of Bach's 'Goldberg Variations'. She felt that she needed something pure, exacting, to listen to, with the emotion well under control.

Then his mobile phone rang. She had noticed that, although he kept it with him most of the time, he used it as little as possible.

The roads here were tricky; he pulled into a layby to answer.

'. . .Nice to hear from you, Professor O'Brien. . . Yes, I would indeed. . . I think I can manage that. . . This evening, then. Look forward to seeing you.'

He clicked off the phone and looked grimly at Zanne. 'Professor O'Brien, over from California. He's read a couple of my papers; could we get together as he has something that might interest me. Only he flies back in two days.'

'Where is he at present?'

'Birmingham. I'll sort things out at the hall and drive down this afternoon.' They were parting again.

He drove her straight to her surgery—she'd said she didn't want to be late. When he stopped he looked at her uncertainly. 'I have to go, Zanne.'

'Well, of course you do,' she said breezily. 'Don't worry, I'll still be here when you get back.'

'You will. Good. Zanne, about last night. . .'

'Last night was last night. Now I've got patients waiting for me. Goodbye, Neil. Hope the Birmingham trip is worthwhile.' She leaned forward to kiss him briskly on the cheek and then marched inside.

She didn't turn round, but she could feel him staring at her. He was at a loss; he didn't know what she was doing.

She knew exactly what she was doing. In a tortured way she was glad to see him leave. She had to remember that he would never settle. This call was from a professor in Birmingham; the next might be from an expedition leader in Alaska. But it hurt to see the expression on his face.

As she opened the door to her bedroom she heard the first determined drops of rain splattering on her window. After the early sun the sky had turned grey, and lowering clouds had threatened rain. Now the rain had started, and in earnest. There was no wind, just a steady sullen downpour. Zanne's mouth curled. The weather matched her mood.

She was happy to change into her uniform. As ever, it made her feel certain of who she was—a professional doing a job she was trained for. Alan Mitchell had promised to cover while she was away, but apparently he hadn't been needed.

Two patients were waiting for her—both were managers. One, Dave Smartt, she'd spoken to before and had tried to warn that he was overdoing things. Dave was a salesman, brash and self-confident. She couldn't remember the name of the other man but she frowned when she looked at him. She recognised the signs— the bags under the eyes and the lines round the mouth. This man was in pain.

Dave was first; he shouldn't take too long. She had to hide a smile when he tried to walk. He wanted to limp, but both legs were causing him agony.

She sat him in the chair. 'Blisters?' she asked. 'After all I told you?'

Cautiously he unlaced his boot. 'On this foot. I know what you said, but we were moving so well I didn't want to ask the group to stop so I could retie my boot.'

'I hope they're grateful,' she said. 'Let's have a look.'

She winced when she saw the area of almost raw flesh round his heel and the side of his foot. He must have been in agony. Carefully she cleaned the red, inflamed area, then pressed it. The skin was broken. 'I think this is infected. I'll phone the doctor and ask him to prescribe you some antibiotics. But, for now, I'll put on some cooling ointment. Now, what about the other leg?'

'It was towards the end of yesterday. We were coming down the hillside, I put my foot in a bog and fell forward. I think I wrenched my knee.'

'Go behind that screen and take your trousers off.' Dave must have been feeling the pain. He didn't make any humorous cracks.

The knee was bruised and swollen. She probed it gently, paying attention to his hiss of pain. 'Were you able to continue walking?'

'After a while, yes. The swelling only started later.'

'So you rested it last night?'

He looked uncomfortable. 'Well, actually, no. I didn't want to be a party-pooper so I took three aspirin and went to the pub with the others. But then this morning. . .'

'I see,' she said, deciding that it wasn't her job to be judgemental. 'Now, you can move it. . .gently. . . good. Right, Dave, I think all you've got is a sprain. It's quite a nasty one and I'm sure it's painful, but since you seem to have full movement I don't think there's anything broken. You didn't do it any good last night.'

She rose and fetched a piece of paper. 'The treatment is ICER.' she wrote for him. 'Ice, compression, elevation and rest. Go back to your room, put an ice compress on your knee, lie with it propped up—and *rest*!'

'But tonight there's a. . .'

'Not for you there isn't. Dave, if you don't do as I say, it'll get worse.'

'All right,' he said, crestfallen. 'I'll follow orders.' She wondered if he would.

Her next patient introduced himself as Gregory Slade. He limped slightly and was obviously in real pain. 'I think I've strained my back,' he explained as he lowered himself cautiously into her chair. 'Can you give me anything to rub on it?'

'Possibly. When did this come on?'

He shrugged. 'A couple of days ago. I wasn't carrying anything and I did take things easy, as you said.'

'How do you feel in yourself? Happy? Full of beans?'

'Well, I haven't felt all that brilliant, no.'

She took his temperature. 'You've got a slight fever; that's probably why you're feeling ill. What exactly happened?'

'Well, I just suddenly doubled up with this amazing pain in my side. Then, after a while, it went away.'

'Doesn't sound like a strained back,' she said. 'Could you take your shirt off?'

There was a small area where the pain was concentrated. When she looked more closely she could see that the skin was inflamed, as if a rash was appearing. 'Have you ever had chicken pox, Mr Slade?'

'Yes, when I was young I. . . No, I haven't!'

'I'm afraid you have, Mr Slade. You've got shingles—herpes zoster. I'll get the doctor in this afternoon to have a look and he might prescribe an antiviral drug. Otherwise, bathing in cool water and paracetamol for the pain. Now, is there anyone pregnant in your family, or have you been in contact with anyone pregnant?'

'No.' Mr Slade didn't seem very pleased.

'Well, you know enough to keep away. Now go and rest, and I'll get the doctor to call at your room.'

She phoned Alan, who said he'd come round in the afternoon. Then she went to the window and stared at the incessant rain. Not a good day to be out.

John Brownlees called on the internal phone. He was ordering in all groups; the weather forecast said that the rain would persist for at least twenty-four hours. Winds would develop on higher ground. Zanne had intended to go out with one of the groups—now it wasn't possible.

She wandered restlessly about her little domain, wanting neither to work nor to look for company. She knew exactly what was wrong—but she forced herself not to think about Neil. She had made up her mind how to deal with their affair. She would live with the pain.

However, she was pleased when Alan Mitchell turned up. He confirmed that Gregory Slade did have shingles. Then he looked mournful until she took pity on him and made a cafetière of coffee for them to share.

'I've had some good news,' she said, concealing the fact that she was also miserable, 'I've been accepted for medical school.'

'Zanne, congratulations! You'll make a wonderful doctor.' He thought a minute. 'The pity is that you're a wonderful nurse. Oh, well.' He beamed. 'If you're thinking of doing GP training when you finish—let me know. Now, I mean that.'

'That's an offer I'll certainly bear in mind,' she said sincerely.

'Good. Corporal Williams, by the way, has won his fight with the social services. He won't go into sheltered accommodation. Apparently, your Dr Calder phoned up the headquarters of his old regiment and told them the situation. They scouted round and found a brigadier who's retired to a farm fifteen miles away. He's offered the corporal an old caravan on his farm. It's warm and it's got electricity and water. The corporal's thinking about it—but I suspect he'll accept.'

'Neil did that?' she asked.

'He's a very thoughtful fellow. Gave me the old soldier's medals to keep safe.'

There were facets to Neil's character that she'd never dreamed of. And, each time she came across one, it unsettled her.

There was the subdued beep of a mobile phone, and Alan took his out and looked at it with distaste. 'Very handy, these things,' he said. 'I hate them. Hello, Alison. What's the problem?'

Two minutes later he put the offending machine back in his pocket and said, 'Alison Turner, our midwife.

This afternoon she was going up to Black Ghyll to check on Gill Stather—she's a primigravida. But Alison's got a problem with a neonate in the village so wants me to go up to see Gill. Alison tried to phone the farm to say she wasn't coming, but the telephone lines are down. It's the rain, as usual.'

He grinned at her. 'Fancy a rainy trip out to the country? It's lonely up there and Gill might like to see a female face.'

'Love it,' Zanne said promptly. 'Remember—I've just seen a man with shingles.'

'No problem. I've checked the medical notes; she's had chickenpox.'

It would take her out of herself; give her something to concentrate on. 'Are we likely to need anything medical?'

'Nothing whatsoever. This is largely a social call. Anyway, I've got my boxes.'

In the back of his car Alan kept two large boxes, holding almost everything he might need in a medical emergency. 'Some of it I've only used once in thirty years,' he told Zanne, 'but was I glad of it that once.'

Zanne phoned Reception to tell them where she was going, and collected an armful of magazines that Mrs Stather might like. Then she changed into her hard-weather gear—boots, trousers, heavy sweater and long anorak. This wasn't like a doctor's or a midwife's visit in a town.

Finally, the dash to Alan's car—a Land Rover Discovery—and they were off.

Alan wasn't as good a driver as Neil, but he was experienced at this kind of driving. First they negotiated a maze of little lanes, moving ever nearer the hills—

now nothing but grey smudges. Rain battered on the car roof, and squirted upwards from under the wheels. Then she had to get out to open a gate. Here they were on a concreted path, now a river of muddy water.

There were more gates and cattle-grids, then they were on the open moor. The farm path climbed the side of a deep valley towards Black Ghyll Head. There was a precipitous fall to their right and an upward slope to their left.

Cautiously Alan crawled round a corner, an outcrop of wet stone. A stream ran through a culvert under the path here. But the culvert was blocked, and the full force of the swollen stream was crashing against the side of the road—finding whatever route it could.

Alan and Zanne got out to inspect. It should be all right. Then Alan inched the car forward. They had almost crossed when the back of the car dropped sickeningly. For a moment they were still, but then the four-wheel drive pulled them to safety.

When they were certain that they were safe they stopped and walked back to see what had happened. A section of the road, loosened by the driving water and strained by the weight of their car, had slid down into the valley. 'We'll not get back that way,' Alan said. 'And it's the only road in.'

They drove on. Soon, at the valley head, they saw the farm—a grey building in a grey landscape, a wisp of smoke coming from the chimney.

'It's a lonely place,' Zanne said.

'Just Adam Stather and his wife. The nearest place is old Grainger's farm about a mile away. He lives on his own.' Alan chuckled. 'He's deaf. When I tried to get him a hearing aid he said there was no point—he didn't want to listen to people anyway.'

'There's nobody else round here?'

'Nobody. Nobody for miles.'

They parked the car and dashed through the rain to the farm porch. Someone must have been watching because the door was already open for them. Zanne saw a tall man with deep blue eyes, dressed in a farmer's rough clothes.

'Doctor Mitchell, it's good to see you,' he said calmly. 'Though we were expecting the midwife. Do come in.'

They stepped inside. Zanne glanced round and saw a room with stone floor, a great fire and odd pieces of beautifully polished heavy furniture. It was a room with dignity.

A blonde girl stepped into the room, obviously heavily pregnant. She smiled shyly. 'Hello, Dr Mitchell,' she said. 'I think I'm starting labour.'

Alan stepped back from the bed. 'Contractions ten minutes apart,' he said. 'No trouble at all. It's just that some babies have no sense of time. This one wasn't due for another four weeks.'

Gill's face was still contorted from the pain of the last contraction, but she managed a smile of triumph. 'I'm going to have my baby here,' she said. 'Well, it's what I wanted.'

Alan patted her wrist. 'There are arrangements to be made,' he said. 'We'll just go and have a word with Adam.'

It was all a little unreal to Zanne. Although she'd worked in the country for quite some time now, she hadn't quite realised how remote some of it was.

'You know the telephone line is down, and half the road has slipped away?' Alan asked Adam calmly.

'Situation just about normal,' Adam said equally calmly.

'So we can't get an ambulance up here. I could organise a helicopter from the RAF Rescue, but I don't think that it's that kind of emergency. At least, not yet.'

'I was born here; my father was born here; my grandfather was born here. It would please me if this baby was born here too. But Gill's safety and comfort are the most important things.'

'I think we can cope. Now, first thing, take my mobile phone and climb to the top of the hill. You won't be in a radio shadow there, and you can get a message through. Phone my surgery, tell them what's happening and get them to phone Lawiston Hall. Make it clear that there's no emergency. We can cope on our own.'

'I'll do that. And I'll go to Grainger and ask him to see to my beasts. Then I can help you if necessary.' Adam went upstairs to speak to his wife.

'I've never done anything like this,' Zanne said slightly apprehensively. 'I've helped deliver—but always in a hospital. With backup.'

'This is a perfectly normal business. Gill isn't ill— she's pregnant. There are absolutely no retrograde signs. Look at how calm Adam is. He's close to his animals; he knows Mother Nature will take care of everything.'

'I hope we can help her a bit,' Zanne muttered.

They decided that the baby should be born downstairs in the living-room. It was the easiest room to keep warm and next door to the bathroom. Zanne sat

upstairs with Gill while Alan prowled round downstairs, setting out the contents of his boxes and making
decisions.

'I think I want to walk round a bit,' Gill gasped.
'Ow! This isn't just painful—it's uncomfortable.'

Zanne helped her out of bed. 'When your husband
returns we'll get him to help you,' she said. 'He won't
be long.'

'I'm glad he's going to be with me.'

In fact, Adam reappeared ten minutes later. He had
washed and changed out of his outdoor clothes, and
Zanne couldn't help noticing what a handsome man he
was. 'How are you, love?' he asked.

Zanne glanced at Gill, and saw the love in her eyes.
'I'm glad you're back,' she said. 'It hurts!'

'Sit on the end of the bed and lean against me.' He
sat next to her, put an arm round her and stroked her
back with the other hand. 'Soon it will be over,' he
said. 'Soon the pain will be over and we'll have a
baby—small, squealing but perfect. You can think
about names if you like. But the pain won't be too
bad. . . Now. . .'

For a moment Zanne listened, fascinated, to his deep
gentle voice. It was hypnotic; she could see Gill
relaxing and drawing comfort from his presence. 'I'll
just go downstairs,' she said, but they didn't notice
her going.

On Alan's instructions Adam had brought a bed into
the living-room. Now the room had to be prepared.
The rugs were taken from the stone floor and a large
plastic sheet was spread over the bed. Zanne put a
bigger bulb into the overhead light, and arranged two

bedside lamps so that they could be used, if necessary, for internal examinations.

'The water here's from a spring up the hillside,' Alan said. 'Probably better than our tap water—but boil plenty anyway.' She did this, then found a plain table in the kitchen, scrubbed it and set it by the bedside.

Alan opened the bag containing the delivery equipment. Zanne looked inside it, took out the Penlom bag, which could be used to help a baby to breathe, and hoped that they wouldn't have to use it.

'Where's the baby to go?' she asked.

'There's a cot in the back room. You can put it in the corner over there. Now, remember, having a baby can be a messy business. There are a couple of aprons there, and we want a lot of dressings. They're all ready in that bag.'

She looked at him quizzically. 'You're quite enjoying yourself, aren't you?'

He laughed. 'Being a doctor was more like this when I started. Yes, I'm afraid I am. Now, I think it's time we had the patient downstairs. This room's quite warm enough and there are no draughts.'

They sat Gill on the bed, propped up with cushions, and Alan made a quick internal examination. 'Cervix is fully dilated. Head well down and in a good position,' he said with satisfaction. 'Everything is going smoothly. We shouldn't need to send for the emergency services. How d'you feel, Gill?'

'All right,' Gill gasped. 'I feel all right.' Adam moved back to her side, and wiped her hot face with a cloth.

Some day I hope some man looks at me like that, Zanne thought. And I'll look back at him like Gill is doing. Then she told herself to stop dreaming—she had a job to do.

There was another hoarse cry from the bed. 'D'you want entonox for the pain?' Zanne asked. 'We have a cylinder here. It's quite safe, you know.'

'I know. The midwife told me. But I'm all right for a while.'

Alan placed a Pinard's stethoscope on Gill's raised abdomen, and listened intently. 'Baby's heartbeat is fine,' he reported.

'Could I listen?' Adam asked. 'He's kicked me in bed often enough; now I want to hear him.'

He leaned over and listened. 'It sounds good,' he said to his wife. 'Heartbeat like a hammer.'

The contractions were much closer together now; it wouldn't be too long before the baby was born. 'There's paperwork everywhere, all the time,' Alan said. 'We'll have to fill in a partogram. There's one in my bag there, Zanne.'

She fetched the form and filled it in as Alan dictated. Foetal heart rate, temperature of mother, pulse, blood pressure—all the details of the birth were monitored and recorded at fifteen-minute intervals.

Gill still refused the entonox. The pain was almost constant now; the baby was almost there but as long as she could hold her husband's hands she seemed to be able to cope. She would give birth sitting up at the head of the bed, propped against the great wooden headboard by cushions.

Then it was time. 'Now push, Gill, push,' Alan instructed, and her face contorted with the effort. Zanne stood by, watching with Adam.

Then there was one last cry from Gill—of exultation,

rather than pain. Alan reached and gathered. 'Now, look what we have here, Gill. A fine baby girl.' In the suddenly silent room they all heard—a wail.

Zanne took the baby, wrapped her in the cloths put ready and gave her a quick wipe of the face. Meanwhile, Alan deftly fitted clamps to the cord.

'There's no need to check for respiratory effort,' he said. 'I can hear she's doing fine.' Baby Stather didn't seem too pleased at being forced into this world.

Her mother asked every mother's question, 'Is she all right?'

'Perfectly all right,' Alan reassured Gill. 'Here, hold her.'

Zanne gave the baby to her mother. She thought she'd never forget the smile on Gill's face. Like so many mothers, Gill checked the tiny fingers and toes and examined the crumpled face with its cap of dark hair. 'If it was a boy I was going to call him Adam,' she said. 'We haven't thought of a girl's name.'

'What about Eve?' Alan suggested with a smile.

Gill put her baby to her breast at once, and this had the desired effect—soon the placenta emerged. Alan checked for bleeding and listened to the pulse in the cord before clamping it. Then blood pressure, temperature, pulse—all were fine.

'You three stay here together for a while,' Alan said. 'Have a rest. Zanne and I will go to the kitchen for a cup of tea.'

'I made some sandwiches,' Adam said.

'We will give her an Apgar score of ten,' Alan said as Zanne made tea. 'Maximum of two points each for heart rate, respiratory effort, muscle tone, reflex response to stimulus and colour.' He entered the score on the partogram.

'I thought most doctors were satisfied with nine,' she said.

'This is a special baby; it was a wonderful birth. I wish they were all like that.'

'She had no entonox at all,' Zanne marvelled. 'I know she felt the pain, but it didn't seem to matter.'

'That was Adam. A caring, loving husband is worth no end of medical expertise, Zanne.'

'A caring, loving husband,' she repeated. 'Can you get them on the National Health?'

To Zanne's amazement it was only nine o'clock. There seemed to have been such a lot fitted into the day. Alan and Adam ate in the kitchen while Zanne attended to Gill, washing her and remaking the bed. Then there were other tasks before Gill could safely be left. The baby was examined again and then placed on her back in the cot by her mother's side. Gill drank a little tea but refused any food.

There was an argument which Zanne won. Alan and Adam would sleep upstairs, and she would cat-nap in front of the fire in the kitchen in a chair. 'Gill needs a nurse now, not a doctor. So she's my patient and this is my ward. She needs a bit of quiet without husbands and doctors thumping round. Don't worry, I'll get you up if necessary.'

Alan nodded. 'Probably a good idea. But I want to be woken in four hours anyway. Just to check.'

The two men went upstairs to make beds.

And at ten o'clock there came a tap on the front door.

*　　*　　*

In the odd minute she'd had spare that afternoon, Zanne had noticed that the rain had never stopped. Who could it possibly be? She opened the door. There was Neil Calder.

He was unslinging a large rucksack. He was, of course, drenched, but she noticed that he was dressed in the best hard-weather gear. With a frown he said, 'I'll leave these wet things in the porch and then come in, if I may.'

'Of course,' she gulped.

A minute later he was inside, clad in the tracksuit he'd been wearing under his heavy waterproof outer garments. 'Mother and child doing well?' he asked, and bent to look at the now-sleeping baby.

Gill smiled at her unexpected guest. 'She's beautiful,' she said. 'It's nice of you to call.'

Alan and Adam came downstairs and there was a flurry of introductions and explanations. 'I heard what was happening,' Neil explained, 'so I thought I'd walk up with some stuff that might be useful.' He took a package from his rucksack and handed it to Alan. 'This is from the midwife.'

He shook hands with Adam, congratulated him and said, 'I thought there might be cause for celebration so I bought you a bottle of champagne.'

'Drink it now,' Gill said from her bed. Alan went to fetch glasses.

'Messages,' Neil continued. 'The midwife will be here as soon as she can, but thinks that you, Alan, are reasonably competent.'

'I wish she'd write that down,' Alan commented.

'Your mother, Gill, will come up tomorrow and get here as soon as she can.'

'She'll be sorry she missed the birth of her first grandchild,' Gill said.

'And the Highways Department will start work on the road as soon as possible.'

Alan returned with the glasses. Zanne said firmly, 'Two more minutes in here and then all into the kitchen. Gill needs her sleep. In fact, you all need sleep.'

Gill had one mouthful of champagne and then drank tea. She was left alone with her husband for five minutes while the others drank their champagne in the kitchen. Then Adam rejoined them and there was another argument about who should sleep where. Eventually Zanne laid the law down again. Neil had brought a sleeping-bag, so he should sleep in the kitchen with her. There was a couch.

Alan and Adam went to bed. Zanne made up the fire in the living-room, had one last check of mother and baby and then turned out all the lights but one shaded one in a corner. Then she sat quietly until the alteration in Gill's breathing told her that she was asleep. She slipped back into the kitchen and closed the door.

Neil was sitting by the kitchen range, sombre-faced. 'First thing,' she told him. 'One loud word and you're out sleeping with the sheep.'

He whispered back, 'I gather I'm not entitled to any nurse's loving care.'

'You're certainly not. What are you doing here, anyway?'

'I was worried about the situation. Worried about you.'

'There was no need. Why aren't you in Birmingham?'

He reached for the champagne bottle, and poured

another glass. 'Professor O'Brien phoned and cancelled our arrangement. He couldn't get to Birmingham because of the weather. I turned back and found you'd disappeared. When the phone call came about you being stranded here nobody seemed to be bothered but me.'

'Why are you angry with me?' she asked curiously.

'Because you put yourself at risk. I drove up to where the road had slipped. You could have been killed if you'd rolled down there!'

'It wasn't too bad when we crossed,' she said. 'Anyway, what right have you to get angry at what I do?' She was angry at him for being angry at her. 'I can look after myself.'

'You can look after yourself!' She thought she had never heard anyone shout so quietly.

'Do you think about how people who love you might feel when you put yourself in danger?'

He grabbed her by the shoulders, so hard that she could feel his fingers squeezing her flesh. 'That's different!' he said.

'Is it? How?'

He held her a moment longer, then his hands dropped. He turned and went to the kitchen window, then drew the curtain aside so that he could peer out. The rain still thudded on the glass.

After a while he came and sat by her again. He took her unresisting hand and held it in his. 'I'm a bit old for self-knowledge,' he said, 'but I'm just realising that I've been truly selfish.'

'I think you have got a lot of bad characteristics,' she said, 'but I wouldn't say selfishness is one of them.'

'I've always enjoyed a risk, putting myself into

danger. Sometimes risks which normal people would think stupid. And I rarely thought about the effect this could have on people who loved me. How it could hurt them.'

'You mean people like your parents?'

'Well, yes. But also. . .'

From next door there came the quietest of cries, and instantly the creak of the bed as Gill rolled over to look at her baby.

'I must go,' said Zanne.

When she returned twenty minutes later there was Neil, cocooned in his sleeping-bag, obviously fast asleep.

Zanne made herself a cup of instant coffee.

CHAPTER TEN

ZANNE was awakened by someone in the kitchen—
someone who'd been there for some time. There was
the smell of toast and coffee. Her eyes flicked open
and she saw Adam leaning over her, offering her a cup
of coffee.

'I should do that,' she said, trying to struggle out of
her remarkably comfortable chair.

He pressed her back. 'I'm a hill farmer; I get up
early and I want to feel useful. Here, drink this.'

'Are Gill and the baby all right?'

'Perfectly all right. Dr Mitchell's in there with them
and I've taken Gill some breakfast.'

She glanced round the couch; it was empty but for
a neatly folded sleeping-bag. 'Where's Neil?'

'Sitting outside having his coffee. The weather's
changed again, so why don't you join him?'

She glanced at the window. No one could ever be
bored with the Lakeland weather—yesterday's rain had
disappeared and there was a glorious sun. 'I think I'll
just sit here for a minute,' she said.

As she sipped her coffee she collected her thoughts.
Last night she had done as instructed, and roused Alan
after his four hours' sleep. He had come down, checked
on mother and baby and told her that it was her turn
to sleep. When she'd protested that she was fine, he'd
told her that an overtired nurse would make mistakes.
So she'd wrapped herself in a blanket, settled in her

chair and closed her eyes—just for a few minutes. And had slept for hours, it seemed.

She went next door to see the baby feeding, Alan watching happily. The remains of Gill's breakfast were by the bed. She felt guilty. 'Someone's been doing my job,' she said.

Alan looked smug. 'No demarcation here. Besides, you needed your sleep.'

Zanne moved to the side of the bed. 'Anything you think you need, Gill?'

Gill looked up with the doe-eyed look typical of nursing mothers. 'If it's possible I'd like a bath at some time,' she said, 'but otherwise I'm fine.'

Zanne patted her on the shoulder and walked out.

She refilled her coffee-cup and opened the door into the yard. Neil was sitting on a wall, cup in hand, looking down the valley. She walked over and sat beside him.

Before them the valley of Black Ghyll dropped away. With the sun high in the sky, it was now all a fresh green with the silver threads of over-full streams bouncing to the valley bottom.

Neil hadn't shaved, and looked unlike his normal well-kept self. But when he turned to look at her there was the same lurch inside her that she knew she'd never lose.

'The air's like champagne this morning,' he said. 'Sitting here, I wonder why people ever want to live anywhere else.'

'There can be problems,' she pointed out.

'There speaks the voice of gloomy reason. I looked in, by the way; mother and baby appear to be doing well'

'Yes.' She thought about the birth the previous

evening. 'I've got a suspicion that if we hadn't been there Adam would have managed perfectly well on his own. So much for our training and our medical expertise.'

He nodded. 'Childbirth's a natural process. I've been called in to help women in labour in various odd bits of the world. And in each case I've spent my time watching as the local midwife did very well without me. It's a bit humbling.'

They sat together peacefully while she tried to think of a way to introduce a more serious topic. Perhaps first thing in the morning wasn't a good time but, then, what time was good?

'Last night,' she said, 'we were having a conversation when we were interrupted. And when I came back you'd gone to sleep.' It sounded like an accusation. She supposed it was.

'Last night was certainly memorable. But not half as memorable as the night before.'

She hoped he thought that the sudden pinkness in her face came from the breeze. 'Don't avoid the question,' she said. 'Just for once in your life you were being honest—with yourself, that is.'

He didn't reply at first, and she wondered if she'd offended him. No matter, it was a truthful remark.

When eventually he did speak his voice was casual. 'Last night I was tired; perhaps I said things I hadn't fully thought through. I think it would be a good thing for me not to say any more right now. Would you like some more coffee?'

Thoroughly irritated, Zanne snapped, 'No. I'll go and see if Gill is ready for her bath now.'

'Very good. Adam and I will go and see what that slipped road looks like.'

Zanne marched inside in an unmitigated bad temper.

The baby was sleeping and Alan thought it an excellent idea for Gill to have her bath. Zanne ran it, then went to help Gill out of bed. As she might have guessed, there was no need. Gill was quite capable of movement.

'You've got your strength back quickly,' Zanne said. 'D'you feel perfectly all right?'

'A bit sore, of course. But otherwise fine. This country life is good for you.'

In spite of her protestations, Zanne helped Gill into the bath. Then she stayed to chat. If she could concentrate on Gill's life, she wouldn't have to think about that man outside.

'I never left Coventry until I was twenty-one,' Gill explained. 'Then I came here for a holiday and met Adam.'

Although she was angry with the world in general, Zanne couldn't help but be moved by the sweet smile on Gill's lips.

'You can guess the rest,' Gill went on. 'My mother was horrified when she came here at first; she's never been further than ten minutes from Sainsbury's in her life. But she gets on well with Adam and now she's talking of retiring here.'

Zanne felt a swift dart of jealousy. *Her* mother had got on well with Neil. 'People can adapt,' she said hopefully. 'People can change. . . What's that noise?'

'There's a car coming up the valley,' said Gill.

Alison Turner, the midwife, was not well pleased. She looked disapprovingly at Zanne's sweater and trousers, and whipped a white apron round her own pristine blue uniform. 'I would like to examine my patient now, Nurse,' she said. 'I will call you if I need you.'

Alison was in her late fifties and had an air of tremendous efficiency. She obviously took the birthing of a baby on her patch without her being present as a personal affront. Yet when she turned to Gill it was obvious that there was a regard between the two. 'You should have waited for me,' she accused. Hiding her smile, Zanne slipped out.

'Suddenly I feel redundant,' Alan said. 'My medical skills aren't needed here.' He introduced her to a newcomer, a young man dressed in the blue overalls of a mechanic.

'This is Harry Ransom,' he said. 'Harry works in our local garage, but his great interest is what are called ATVs—All Terrain Vehicles. He likes to pretend a car is really a horse. When she heard a baby was being born here without her assistance, the midwife persuaded him to get her here.'

' ''Persuaded'' is the wrong word,' Harry put in. 'How about ''threatened'' or ''blackmailed''?'

Alan grinned. 'Alison was there when Harry was born,' he said. 'Anyway, I'll have one last check on Gill and the baby and then Harry will take the three of us back. We're not needed here any more.'

With a sniff, the midwife admitted grudgingly that the job appeared to have been done adequately under the circumstances. But they certainly weren't needed any longer. She had brought her bag, and would stay for a while. Alan would see to it that the road was mended—and quickly.

'No problem,' Alan said.

'You will come and visit us?' Gill asked Zanne. 'I feel as if we've been through something momentous together. And bring Dr Calder with you.'

'I'll certainly come,' Zanne promised, 'but Dr Calder's movements tend to be—erratic.'

'I'm sure you'll be seeing a lot of him,' Gill said placidly.

There were a few last-minute arrangements to be made and then they said goodbye to Adam. Zanne noticed with some interest that a bond appeared to have formed between Adam and Neil, and they promised to keep in touch. This irritated her too.

Then they were off in Harry's wonder vehicle. Alan sat in the seat in the front, and Zanne and Neil were cramped together in the back. It wasn't a comfortable ride. The car had started life as a Land Rover, and Harry had modified it. When they came to where the road had fallen into the valley, Harry merely turned right. They appeared to climb vertically up what Zanne thought was a cliff with grass on. Then they surged wheel-deep through the stream and turned down onto the road again.

'Thanks, Harry,' Alan said. 'But now I'll beg a lift from Neil. My car's at the farm. I'll be round this afternoon to borrow something.'

'See you all.' And Harry was gone in a spray of mud.

Neil had borrowed one of the hall's Land Rovers; Alan and Zanne climbed in and he drove them sedately back. He first dropped Zanne at the hall, then ran Alan down to his practice.

Zanne, of course, had to report in to John Brownlees. It was still quite early; she'd be able to run her own morning surgery. John was pleased that she was back, and pleased that she'd been able to help.

'I know Adam Stather,' he said. 'He's a good man. Used to be a great rock-climber but gave it up when he got married. Remind me to ask him if we can use his farm for one of our expeditions.'

'You're an old twister,' Zanne told him.

She had a bath, changed into uniform and then it was time for surgery. There was nothing much of interest. Afterwards she felt a great sense of anticlimax. There was nothing much to look forward to in her life. Even the prospect of medical training didn't thrill her so much. It's reaction; you're just tired, she told herself, and tried to lose herself in paperwork.

After ten minutes she put down her pen in disgust. She just couldn't interest herself in estimating and ordering the medical stores for the next three months. It wasn't the excitement and fatigue of the last twenty-four hours. It was Neil Calder.

She was in love with him. As that film title said, truly, madly, completely—or something like that. When he was around she couldn't keep her eyes off him; when he was away she thought of him constantly.

She could have coped if he *had* stayed away. But he wouldn't; he kept turning up. She loved his company, loved it when they did things together, even if it was only to drink coffee overlooking a valley.

But she wanted more. Not only the physical side of their love—though she felt warm when she remembered the sheer extent of her passion—but togetherness. She wanted to share her life with him. And he was a wanderer. Didn't he know what he was doing to her?

*　　*　　*

That afternoon Neil phoned her. The sound of his voice brought equal pleasure and pain.

'Recovered from your ordeal?' he asked.

Zanne forced herself to be light-hearted. 'What ordeal? I thoroughly enjoyed myself. It taught me that you don't need hospitals for medicine.'

'I know that—it's a trade secret. Anyway, would you like to come on a little mystery trip tonight? I've had some good news and I want to share it with you.'

She knew that she should refuse. The pain would only be harder when he went. 'What good news?' she asked.

'I'm not going to tell you yet. A bit of anticipation is good for everyone.'

'You're annoying. At least tell me what to wear.'

'Mystery trip, mysterious good news. Wear anything you like. What about that outfit you wore when we went to the Red Lion?'

'All right,' she said gracelessly.

'I'll pick you up a bit earlier tonight. While there's still plenty of light. Bye!'

He rang, she thought, which I suppose is what I wanted. And now I feel worse than ever.

She was in a fretful mood when he picked her up and he was imperturbable, which made things worse than ever. As requested, she wore the black and white outfit. He arrived in blazer and flannels.

'Where are we going?' she asked sharply, once the Jaguar had purred out of the drive.

Airily he waved his arm. 'It's a balmy evening so I got Oscar to make us up a picnic. Once aboard the lugger and the maid is mine. We're going out on the boat again.'

'Hmm,' said Zanne, remembering what happened last time—and what hadn't happened.

But once aboard his boat she lost herself in the beauty of the surroundings. After yesterday's great storm, the sky now was the deepest of blues. White-sailed yachts skimmed past them. They motored quietly, the engine making hardly a sound. Slowly the wooded hills around them slid past, and slowly her mood calmed.

Neil was responsive to her. He said very little, smiling at her and waiting for her jangling nerves to settle. And, finally, they ran ashore in the lee of a little island. He cut the motor.

'We've been here before,' she said, 'only it was dark.'

'We have indeed,' he agreed. 'I thought we might lay some ghosts; wipe out a couple of memories.'

'So you're not expecting a full repeat of last time?'

'Heaven forbid,' he shuddered, and he looked so injured that she had to giggle.

From a cool-box he'd brought on board he pulled a bottle of champagne. 'Hope you're not getting tired of this stuff,' he said, 'but I was instructed to buy it and, if possible, share with you. This is not my treat, I will certainly be paid for the bottle.'

She was intrigued. Who possibly could want her to share champagne with Neil? She was pretty certain that it wasn't Adam—he had other things on his mind.

'Don't be aggravating,' she said. 'At the moment my temper's not at its best. Who was it?'

Expertly he popped the cork, poured foaming wine into two glasses. 'As a matter of fact, it was Claudette.

She phoned me this afternoon and left a message. She's done the route. And a crew filmed her. It should be fantastic to watch.'

Zanne looked at him. 'You're genuinely pleased, aren't you?' she said.

'Of course I am; she's a friend.'

She wondered about telling him that many men wouldn't be pleased. 'But something that was once yours you now have to share.'

'So what? It happens to all things. In a couple of years there'll be schoolboys running up it in Wellies.'

'I doubt it,' she said with a shiver.

'Well, we'll see. I wonder what Oscar has put up for us.'

It was pleasant, sitting and eating in the cockpit. The world was passing them by, its only sign the occasional buzz of a car on a distant road. They talked about safe things—a letter from her mother, the progress of his research and her plans to study medicine.

She was fascinated when he talked about his training days. But, for her, the white-hot enthusiasm for medicine had cooled slightly. She wanted more than to be a doctor. She wanted him.

'There's more good news,' he said after they had cleared away. 'I've just had a letter from the Royal Society. They've offered me the chance to go to the Antarctic for a year. There's quite a big research budget so I can continue with the work I'm doing here. And I'll get the chance to do some snow- and rock-climbing.'

'When?' she managed to ask.

'They want me in six weeks. Just enough time to sort things out here.'

'Congratulations,' she said, frozen-faced. 'I'm

very happy for you. It is good news.'

She thought she'd never felt such pain. There was
no excuse—she'd known he would go and she'd tried
to stop herself being pulled in too deeply. But all to
no avail. He would leave her, and the cost of his leaving
felt like nails being raked across her naked soul.

She struggled not to let the bitterness of her feelings
show on her face. Her dignity was important; she must
retain it. She managed to smile at him. His expression
was odd. It was pensive, half-amused.

'*That's* not the good news,' he said. 'The good news
is that I'm not going to go. I turned the offer down
at once.'

She gaped at him. 'You turned it down,' she asked,
confused, 'but why?'

She barely noticed that he'd taken her hand in his.
'It's time to stop wandering. And, anyway, look around
here.' He waved at the surrounding hills. 'I've never
found anywhere as beautiful as the Lakes. Besides
which, there's my house and there's the work at
University of the North.'

His voice became more serious. 'And there's something else—something that you made me realise last
night. I have been selfish. I've ignored the feelings of
those I love.'

Her mouth was dry, and automatically she drank
from her glass of champagne. But she wasn't concentrating—the champagne went down the wrong way and
suddenly she was coughing, spluttering and gasping for
breath as the tears ran down her face. And somewhere
behind her physical discomfort lurked the thought—
this is not showing me in a glamorous light.

He laughed, which enraged her and made her choking worse. Then he moved across to clap her on the back. It hurt, but it did the trick. Her coughing slowly subsided. 'You did that on purpose!' she accused.

'No, I didn't.'

'You did! Now, look at me, I'm a mess. Oh, Neil!'

'If I kiss you will it make you cough again?'

'Don't you dare come near me; don't you dare try to kiss me; I hate you and. . .'

But he did kiss her, and she didn't cough. Her breathing subsided and the spasms in her abdomen disappeared. She decided that she quite liked it.

'What did you mean about the feelings of those you love?' she asked.

'The feelings of one I love, in particular. Your feelings, Zanne. I don't ever want to be parted from you again.'

'But. . .'

He kissed her again. 'You're to train to be a doctor. I'm doing research in the same department. There's a house we can live in at the weekends. Will you marry me, Zanne? I'm going to settle down.'

'Oh, Neil! Of course I will. . .'

The wedding was three months later. Her mother and new husband flew from Canada for the occasion. It wasn't too far to travel from her home town and the University of the North, so the ceremony was held in a little Lakeland church and the reception at Lawiston Hall. Alan Mitchell gave the bride away, and the cake was cut—with a scalpel.

'Where are you going for your honeymoon?' Mary Kelly asked when she had a chance of a few private words with her friend. 'Robert and I had a wonderful time in Switzerland.'

Zanne smiled. 'We're starting as we intend to carry on,' she said. 'We're going to this wonderful house in the Lake District. We're going to have a honeymoon at home. . .'

MILLS & BOON®

Medical Romance™

COMING NEXT MONTH

A GIFT FOR HEALING by Lilian Darcy
Camberton Hospital

Karen Graham's manipulative ex-boyfriend, who was sick
with TB, wanted her back. Guilt-ridden, she had no-one to
turn to except Lee Shadwell. He was more than willing to
offer friendship and support. Karen knew she was loved and
in love, but with which man?

POWERS OF PERSUASION by Laura MacDonald

Nadine vowed to remain immune to the charms of the new
Italian registrar Dr Angelo Fabrielli. But that proved
impossible when he moved into her house—and her heart!
But she refused to be his wife knowing that she could never
give him the one thing he needed most...

FAMILY TIES by Joanna Neil

The new locum, Dr Matthew Kingston, was critical and a
touch too arrogant so Becky Laurens kept her distance.
But that proved difficult when she found him incredibly
attractive. Becky had to end things with her current
boyfriend—but was Matthew willing to take his place?

WINGS OF CARE by Meredith Webber
Flying Doctors

Radio operator, Katy Woods, was secretly in love with
Dr Peter Flint. So when he was trapped during a cyclone
she willingly offered words of comfort. And on his return
Peter made it clear that he wanted Katie! But did he
want commitment?

FREE!

FOUR FREE
specially selected
Medical Romance™ novels
PLUS a FREE Mystery Gift
when you return this page...

Return this coupon and we'll send you 4 Medical Romance novels and a mystery gift absolutely FREE! We'll even pay the postage and packing for you.

We're making you this offer to introduce you to the benefits of the Reader Service™– FREE home delivery of brand-new Medical Romance novels, at least a month before they are available in the shops, FREE gifts and a monthly Newsletter packed with information, competitions, author profiles and lots more...

Accepting these FREE books and gift places you under no obligation to buy, you may cancel at any time, even after receiving just your free shipment. Simply complete the coupon below and send it to:

MILLS & BOON READER SERVICE, FREEPOST, CROYDON, SURREY, CR9 3WZ.

READERS IN EIRE PLEASE SEND COUPON TO PO BOX 4546, DUBLIN 24

NO STAMP NEEDED

Yes, please send me 4 free Medical Romance novels and a mystery gift. I understand that unless you hear from me, I will receive 4 superb new titles every month for just £2.20* each, postage and packing free. I am under no obligation to purchase any books and I may cancel or suspend my subscription at any time, but the free books and gift will be mine to keep in any case. (I am over 18 years of age)

M7XE

Ms/Mrs/Miss/Mr _____
BLOCK CAPS PLEASE

Address _____

_____

_____ Postcode _____

New York Times bestselling author of
Power Play and *Cruel legacy*

POWER GAMES

The arrival of a mysterious woman threatens
a son's manipulative hold over his
millionaire father in PENNY JORDAN'S
latest blockbuster—a supercharged tale of
family rivalries

AVAILABLE IN PAPERBACK
FROM MARCH 1997